THE FORTUNES OF TEXAS

Follow the lives and loves of a complex family with a rich history and deep ties in the Lone Star State

DIGGING FOR SECRETS

A ruse brings six estranged Fortunes to Chatelaine, Texas, to supposedly have their most secret wishes granted. They're thrilled—until they discover someone is seeking vengeance for a long-ago wrong...and turning their lives upside down!

After her husband's death, new mom Esme Fortune's picking up the pieces in Chatelaine. Her little one is a joy, but when it turns out her baby was switched with another at birth, her dream becomes a nightmare. She never expected suave Ryder Hayes, the other baby's father, to become her partner in parenting...and, just maybe, in life?

Dear Reader,

Do you like Valentine's Day? I've always had mixed feelings about the holiday. I love everything about love, but I don't enjoy the typical flowers-and-chocolate celebrations. So when I crafted Ryder and Esme's story, I knew I needed to give them a special way to commemorate the holiday. Especially since their relationship is complicated and enhanced by being new parents to two three-month-old baby boys.

Esme has dreamed of having a family of her own, and she gets that in the most unexpected way when she and Ryder Hayes, the last man she'd think a match for her, choose to raise the sons who were switched at birth together. She and Ryder both have past hurts to overcome, but together they find the love they both crave and the family that can make their dreams come true.

So I hope you'll enjoy their journey to happily-ever-after, along with a perfect Valentine's Day, as much as I enjoyed writing it. Please feel free to find me on Facebook and Instagram—I'd love to virtually hang out with you!

Happy reading!

Michelle

FORTUNE'S BABY CLAIM

Michelle Major

Special thanks and acknowledgment are given to
Michelle Major for her contribution to
The Fortunes of Texas: Digging for Secrets miniseries.

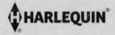

ISBN-13: 978-1-335-59480-8

Fortune's Baby Claim

Recycling programs
for this product may
not exist in your area.

Harlequin Enterprises ULC
22 Adelaide St. West, 41st Floor
Toronto, Ontario M5H 4E3, Canada
www.Harlequin.com

Printed in U.S.A.

Michelle Major grew up in Ohio but dreamed of living in the mountains. Soon after graduating with a degree in journalism, she pointed her car west and settled in Colorado. Her life and house are filled with one great husband, two beautiful kids, a few furry pets and several well-behaved reptiles. She's grateful to have found her passion writing stories with happy endings. Michelle loves to hear from her readers at michellemajor.com.

Books by Michelle Major

Harlequin Special Edition

The Fortunes of Texas: Digging for Secrets
Fortune's Baby Claim

Welcome to Starlight
The Best Intentions
The Last Man She Expected
His Secret Starlight Baby
Starlight and the Single Dad

Crimson, Colorado
Anything for His Baby
A Baby and a Betrothal
Always the Best Man
Christmas on Crimson Mountain
Romancing the Wallflower
Sleigh Bells in Crimson
Coming Home to Crimson

Maggie & Griffin
Falling for the Wrong Brother
Second Chance in Stonecreek
A Stonecreek Christmas Reunion

For additional books by Michelle Major,
visit her website, michellemajor.com.

Prologue

Esme Fortune didn't allow herself to believe in karma because that would mean she'd done something acutely awful to wind up in her current situation.

"You're doing fine," the nurse told her with a gentle pat to her arm before rushing out of the makeshift delivery room that wasn't a room at all—just a tiny alcove on the first floor of County Hospital outside of Chatelaine, Texas.

Another contraction started, bringing a surging wave of pain. At the same time, a flash of lightning followed by a booming clap of thunder shook the window next to her hospital bed.

The lights flickered again, something they'd been doing off and on for the past hour despite the various nurses who popped in and out to monitor the progress of Esme's labor and assure her that the hospital's backup generator was reliable.

At this point, she didn't trust anything—or anyone—other than her sister, Bea, who wasn't here yet. A fallen tree and downed power lines blocked the two-lane highway that led from Chatelaine to the hospital.

But she couldn't worry about her sister right now and instead concentrated on breathing through the pain that ripped through her. One, two, three, four. One, two, three, four...

The first thing she'd done after moving from Houston to Chatelaine a month earlier was to sign up for birthing classes with Bea as her coach. Esme, who'd spent her childhood dreaming of the sort of fairy-tale love that filled the romance novels she devoured, had failed at love and marriage, but she was determined to be the best mother she could.

Her baby would have a wonderful life full of laughter, happiness and no uncertainty about whether they were cherished and adored.

As the contraction subsided, a cold droplet hit her smack dab in the forehead, and she looked up to see water dripping from the ceiling above her. Esme sighed. Clearly, motherhood was not off to an auspicious start.

Who could have predicted that her water breaking would coincide with the late-October storm ravaging the region? It was the kind of storm that happened once in a lifetime—a hundred-year storm, the older neighbor who'd driven her to the hospital ominously reported, glancing at Esme like her situation had somehow predicated the lashing wind and pounding rain.

As it turned out, Esme wasn't the only soon-to-be mother whose baby seemed eager to meet the world in the middle of a torrential downpour. The frantic young woman at the admissions desk reported that four other women were already on the labor and delivery floor of the small hospital—a veritable baby boom in this sleepy region of Texas.

But now they were all crowded into a section of the hospital's OR with hastily constructed fabric partitions separating them after a burst pipe flooded the floor above them.

Esme cradled her stomach and tried to calm her nerves. It would work out. She could handle this. Her late husband might have believed she was weak and ordinary, but she was made of stronger stuff than Seth Watson had claimed. And she'd do anything for the baby she already loved with her whole heart.

A woman's cries from the other side of the divider made Esme's anxiety ratchet up a few levels. But at least she could take solace in the fact that she was managing this unexpected turn of events with more calm than her neighbor, who had been swearing and screeching at staff and the man she kept calling "you big oaf" since Esme had been wheeled in.

"I don't want this," she heard the woman complain in a fierce whisper. "Make it stop. This is your fault, you big oaf! I'll never forgive you."

Esme couldn't hear the guy's response, but his tone was low and calm, especially given the venom being spewed his way. His words might not be comforting to her neighbor, but they had an oddly soothing effect on Esme, and she was grateful to the stranger.

Another contraction roared through her, so she concentrated on activating her own coping techniques once again. As the night drew on, the waves of pain came faster and more intensely, although the woman's shouting and cries drowned out Esme's soft moans.

She hated making any noise. It made her feel like she was losing the battle for control, but the pain slamming through her over and over felt relentless.

A new nurse checked her progress, assuring Esme it was all going according to plan, and she'd be ready to push soon.

No, she wanted to answer. *None of this was part of the plan.* Having a baby alone and raising her child as a single mother was not how she'd envisioned her life.

Was she as ill-equipped to welcome her son or daughter into the world as her neighbor loudly claimed about herself? The difference was the woman next to her had a big oaf at her side.

Esme imagined him broad, hairy and bearing a striking resemblance to the troll under the bridge from the classic children's tale.

How sad was it that even a potentially mean and hungry troll could comfort her now? Clearly, the fairy-tale life she'd imagined had gone very, very sideways.

She lost track of how much time had elapsed, but it felt like hours or days later when the curtain was yanked back to reveal another nurse and an older man who had the commanding air of a doctor.

As they entered the cramped space, tears sprung to Esme's eyes unbidden, but not in response to the pain or the exhaustion that threatened to pull her under like a riptide. She was simply so relieved not to be alone.

For an instant, her gaze was drawn to something over the doctor's shoulder, and she found herself looking into the most piercing set of green eyes she'd ever seen. Esme's eyes were green or hazel, depending on her mood, but the man staring at her had eyes the color of spring grass, vibrant and full of promise.

She had just enough time to register the handsome face surrounding those green eyes, a strong jaw and a full mouth that curved into the barest hint of a smile as he nodded and mouthed, "You've got this." He couldn't possibly be the oaf, or else Esme was delirious with fatigue.

But those three little words spoken silently by a stranger bolstered her resolve in a way that defied logic.

As the nurse pulled the curtain shut, Esme drew in the steadiest breath she could manage.

"Are you ready to meet your baby?" the doctor asked in a reassuring tone, then simultaneously winced and chuckled as another crack of thunder reverberated around them. "Because a child born on a night like this is bound to be special."

Esme swallowed around the emotion clogging her throat, then nodded. "I'm ready," she whispered.

Chapter One

"You aren't alone," Bea reassured Esme three months later as they sat at the small kitchen table in Esme's postage-stamp-size kitchen.

However, she didn't mind the diminutive proportions of her house in one of the older neighborhoods of Chatelaine. There was plenty of room for her and baby Chase, and owning her own home meant the world to her. It was more than she could have imagined in the lonely, shocking months after her husband's death at the beginning of the previous year and the subsequent revelation he'd been cheating on her since the start of their relationship.

She and Seth had married at the courthouse two days after a doctor confirmed the results of the half dozen home pregnancy tests Esme had taken. But within weeks of the wedding, Seth turned distant, traveling almost constantly for his company and leaving her alone in a cramped apartment near the elementary school in Houston, where she taught first grade.

Then she'd discovered he'd been cheating on her since the start of their relationship. And although the betrayal hurt, she'd been determined to try to make the marriage work for the sake of the baby. She'd been scared but not heartbroken and Seth had agreed to go to counseling, but showed no signs of changing his behavior. And Esme had started to wonder if she'd be relegated to the same fate as her mother in an unhappy marriage and if staying the course was truly worth it.

When Seth was killed in a boating accident on the open water near Galveston the day before they were scheduled for their first appointment with the counselor, Esme felt heartbroken for her unborn child, who'd never know his father, but her heart had remained numb. She'd weathered another shock a few weeks later when she'd received a check as the beneficiary of Seth's modest life insurance policy.

He hadn't been the knight in shining armor she'd longed for as a girl, but she would always be grateful for how he'd taken care of her and their child.

"I don't know anything about Seth's family," she told Bea, as if her sister, who knew her better than anyone in the world, didn't understand where her trepidation about this moment originated. "He barely spoke about them, and it was never anything good. For all I know, they could be horrible people." She drew a finger along the edge of the envelope from the DNA testing company, 411 Me. "Remind me why I wanted to do this in the first place?"

"Because Freya gifted it to you, and you're curious." Bea squeezed Esme's trembling hand. "I'm curious as well. For all either of us know, Chase could be related to someone famous."

"Or infamous," Esme muttered and took a small sip of the wine her sister had brought over. "Why do you think Freya did it? Why has she done any of this?" The questions had been pinging around Esme's brain the past two weeks as she waited for the results of the DNA test her late great-uncle's widow, Freya Fortune, had encouraged her to take.

But to be fair, she tended to question every aspect of her life in the middle of the night as she blearily fed Chase, whose understanding of the difference between day and night had been wonky in recent weeks.

So it was difficult to know whether her uncertainty about Freya Fortune and the significant role she now played in the lives of Esme, her siblings and their cousins was justified or simply the workings of her tired and muddled mind.

Bea ran a hand through her flaming red hair. She was eight years older than Esme, and while their faces and eyes were the same shape, Esme had dark hair and green eyes in contrast to Bea's radiant red locks and blue eyes. Of course, Esme was also sporting some new-mom bags under her eyes, thanks to Chase.

"I like to think of Freya as a fairy godmother," Bea said with a smile. "Or our fairy step-great aunt." She drummed her fingers on Esme's table. "I'd always wanted to own a restaurant, but I never would have gotten a chance to open the Cowgirl Café without Freya's generosity. Neither Edgar nor Elias Fortune have the best reputation in Chatelaine—"

"That's putting it mildly," Esme said with a laugh.

Edgar and Elias had run the Fortune silver mine in town. But after overhearing a conversation between their estranged brothers, Wendell and Walter, they'd mistakenly believed their mine might also produce gold. The story Esme had heard after moving to Chatelaine was that the potential of wealth beyond their wildest dreams prompted the brothers to overwork their miners. Their greed led to the unsafe conditions that resulted in a tragic collapse of the mine that killed fifty men, including the foreman, who Edgar and Elias blamed instead of taking responsibility themselves.

She didn't want to believe her grandfather and great uncle had used their wealth to avoid being held accountable, but the brothers had left Chatelaine in disgrace shortly after the accident. They'd resurfaced hours away in Cave Creek, staying long enough for each of them to start a family before disappearing again.

Bea traced a finger along the rim of her wine glass. "If Great-Uncle Elias truly had a change of heart at the end of his life the way Freya claims, her financial support will go a long way in changing what people around here think about our branch of the Fortune family tree. I hope by her sharing what's left of his money with us, we can repair some of the damage our grandfather and great-uncle caused and hopefully make a positive impact on this community."

Esme sighed. "You always make me feel better, sis. Although you're doing much more good for this town with your plan to open a restaurant than I am with the money Freya has given me."

They'd each received a letter from Freya Fortune at the end of last summer explaining that she was their great-uncle's widow and extending an invitation to come to Chatelaine and learn more about their past in the town.

"Look at this little cutie," Bea commanded as she held Esme's phone aloft. The screensaver was a carousel of photos featuring baby Chase. One from the day Esme had brought him home from the hospital bundled in a blue blanket with a knit cap covering his wispy dark hair to several more recent photos documenting him sleeping and his first smile.

"There's nothing more important than devoting yourself to being a mother. You'll return to teaching refreshed and renewed next school year, Es. And the elementary school community will love you just like your former students. Chatelaine is both of our homes now. Asa's, too. He's bound and determined Chase will learn to ride a horse before he even walks."

Esme grinned at the thought of her older brother

finally owning the dude ranch he was working to purchase just outside of town.

"Still…" She tipped her wine glass in her sister's direction, then took another drink. "Don't you think it's strange Freya is taking such an interest in us?"

Bea wrinkled her nose. "Maybe, but I prefer to imagine thanking her with an amazing meal once I open my restaurant. And I'm certain that you're over-thinking it right now as an excuse to avoid opening this report." She picked it up and handed the envelope to Esme. "Let's go, girl. I hope to find out my nephew is secretly related to George Clooney."

At Esme's raised brow, Bea clarified, "George circa hotter *before he was huge but he had great hair and the best broody stare.*"

Esme knew her sister was joking to ease the tension, and as always with the two of them, it worked. She slid one finger under the seal, tore it open and then pulled out the small stack of papers detailing her son's genetic family tree.

As part of the package, she'd also had an opportunity for her own testing, so she started with her results, which were exactly what she'd expected. There were plenty of skeletons in the Fortune closet, but most of those had seen the light of day years earlier—at least the ones that involved Esme's relatives.

She wondered what her grandfather and great-uncle would have thought of this kind of technological advancement if they'd lived long enough to see it. Her mom and dad had been killed in a plane crash five years earlier. While her parents hadn't shared a loving relationship for most of their marriage, she'd never expected to lose them so suddenly and wished they could have been here to meet their grandson.

Esme continued to read, but what the report revealed about her son didn't make any sense.

"What's wrong?" Bea asked. "Don't tell me there's truly someone infamous in Seth's family."

Esme shook her head. Her throat had gone dry as she tried to process what the DNA report meant regarding her son's background.

"There's not one Fortune or anyone from Seth's family listed. Several of them have the last name Hayes. I—I don't understand…"

"Maybe that was his mother's maiden name?" her sister murmured.

"No, her name was Williams. Lana Williams. She died when Seth was in high school, but he still used her name as a password for most of his online accounts. That's the reason I'm sure Hayes isn't right. *None* of this is right."

"Do you think 411 Me inadvertently gave you the wrong report for Chase?" Bea asked. "I mean, otherwise, how can any of this make sense when your results seem valid?"

"I can't explain it, but I had a weird feeling that doing the DNA test was a mistake."

"It has to be a mix-up." Esme's sister grabbed the papers from her. "They're based out of California, and it says customer service is still open. Let's call them and get to the bottom of it."

Bea had to be correct. It must be a technical error.

She'd call, and they'd redo the tests, or maybe, as her sister had suggested, there had been a mix-up, and they would just send her the correct information.

"They better offer a refund for putting me through this headache," she said with a laugh that didn't feel humorous.

"You want me to call?" Bea asked. "I'd be happy to give those people a piece of my mind!"

Esme picked up the phone and punched in the number listed on the report. "Thanks, but I need to be the one to talk to them. I want to hear for myself that it's a mistake because the other option—"

"There *is* no other option." Bea hugged her, and Esme tried to channel her sister's confidence as she waited for someone to answer.

A few minutes later, she explained the situation to the cold and clinical-sounding woman on the other end of the line.

After double checking the results from their database, the woman curtly asked Esme if there was a possibility her child could have been fathered by someone other than the man she believed to be Chase's biological dad.

The question was almost as shocking as initially reading the report. While Esme hadn't been entirely inexperienced when she'd begun seeing Seth, her accidental pregnancy had still made her feel like a naive fool.

But she'd ended things with her only other serious boyfriend a year before meeting her late husband. Serious enough for that sort of intimacy anyway.

The 411 Me representative didn't sound surprised or convinced by Esme's vehement denial.

Clearly, this wasn't the first call the company had received along this vein. After going back and forth several times, Esme finally persuaded the woman she was telling the truth, and the company representative's voice gentled considerably. Only the suggestion she gave Esme landed with all the subtlety of a lead balloon.

Her heart reeled and blood roared between her ears as she thanked the woman and finally ended the call.

"What did she say?" Bea grabbed her hand, but Esme barely registered the touch. "Was it a mistake? Why do you look like you're going to puke? Tell me it's too much wine."

"She said I need to contact the hospital where I gave birth."

Her sister's eyes widened. "Why? Did they mess up something?"

Esme thought back to the chaos of the night Chase was born—rain lashing against the window, lights flickering and the kind nurses who seemed so discombobulated.

Still, the idea of what the 411 Me representative had proposed as an explanation was outside the realm of possibility.

At least, that was what Esme wanted to believe.

"She thinks it's possible that Chase isn't mine." Esme choked out a sob. "There could have been a mistake and…"

She met Bea's concerned gaze and tried to focus

past the tears blurring her vision. It was obvious when her sister understood what she was trying to say because Bea grabbed her shoulders and shook them gently.

"No. Chase is *your* son. We'll go to the hospital right now."

"I'm not going to wake him." Esme wiped a hand over her cheeks. "It's getting late, and I need time to think. I'll call County Hospital in the morning and—"

"They'll have an answer for you," Bea assured her. "One that explains all of this. Do you want me to stay? I can sleep in the spare bedroom so you're not alone."

"Thanks, but it's okay. I'm fine." And even though Bea sat beside her, Esme had never felt more alone.

They talked for a few more minutes, then after another long hug, Bea left, and Esme walked up the stairs and slipped into Chase's nursery.

The crib was lit by the soft glow of a night-light plugged into the wall, and she pressed a hand over her mouth to keep in the cries that threatened to escape.

Her sweet boy slept peacefully on his back, swaddled in a cotton blanket her grandmother had sent after his birth. He looked like a baby burrito, and Esme sank onto the carpet next to the crib, content to watch his chest rise and fall. Chase was her son, she reminded herself.

No test results or mix-up in a lab would change that. Tomorrow, she'd go to the hospital and demand an explanation. Standing up for herself didn't come easily to Esme, but she'd do anything for her baby boy.

After a while, exhaustion got the best of her, but she couldn't bring herself to leave the nursery. She grabbed a blanket and a pillow from the glider in the corner to arrange a makeshift bed on the floor. Then she closed her eyes and commanded her heart to remember that Chase belonged to her—forever.

Chapter Two

Ryder Hayes was determined to be a calm, organized, totally together single dad to his three-month-old son, Noah.

Just not this particular morning.

After staying up past his embarrassingly early bedtime last night to wash and dry dirty bottles, fold laundry and pack his son's extra clothes for the babysitter, he'd almost made it out the door on time.

Then Noah had a diaper blowout—all over Ryder's crisp white button-down. Weren't diapers supposed to hold *in* the poop? Ryder's baby seemed to be a master at pooping sideways, diagonally and with the force of Old Faithful erupting.

Thirty minutes after his planned departure, Ryder clicked Noah's infant seat into the base in the back of his car and headed toward the house of the older woman who watched him daily.

Anna Mitchell was an absolute angel, and he honestly didn't know how he'd manage without her. Although he'd offered to marry his late ex-girlfriend, Stephanie, after discovering she was pregnant, she had wanted nothing to do with marriage—or motherhood, as it turned out.

He shook his head, committed to believing that if a car accident hadn't taken her life a few weeks after Noah's birth, she would have eventually warmed to the idea of being a mom.

From the moment Noah's tiny hand curled around Ryder's finger in the hospital, he'd been a goner—completely smitten with his son. Too bad that loving a baby didn't intrinsically equate to knowing how to care for one. Ryder was doing his best, but most days, it felt like his life was on the brink of collapse in almost all areas.

Speaking of collapse…

He grabbed his phone from where he'd tossed it on the passenger seat, ready to call his father and offer a better excuse than a diaper blowout for why he would be late to the meeting with Hayes Enterprises' senior management team along with several key investors. After deciding to retire in this small town, his dad had made plans to move the headquarters for their family's portfolio of private social clubs and resorts to Chatelaine. Chandler Hayes was ready to give up running the mini empire he'd built but refused to relinquish complete control.

The question was whether Dad would be handing over the reins to Ryder or his brother, Brandon, who was a chip off the old womanizing block and seemed to relish Ryder's struggle to balance his work duties with fatherhood.

Noah's uncle Brandon would have laughed his butt off at the diaper emergency, only Ryder would keep that debacle to himself. Because anything that revealed a perceived weakness could and would be used against him, and he had a son to care for now, entirely on his own. He *needed* this promotion.

Before he could place the call, his phone began to ring. He answered, his heart pounding as he listened to the hospital administrator's cryptic request that he bring Noah to the facility immediately for an urgent meeting with the hospital's attorney.

An attorney—what the hell was that about?

The woman, who identified herself as County Hospital's chief executive, refused to answer the questions Ryder fired off and insisted everything would be explained in person.

His mind raced as he turned the car around and quickly called his father's assistant to explain that an emergency would prevent him from attending the board meeting. Cynthia's voice was tight as she promised to relay the message, and he knew it was cowardly not to call his dad or Brandon directly, but he had more important things to worry about.

Nothing took precedence over Noah, and the fear pounding through Ryder refused to abate no matter how many times he reminded himself that though he might not have a handle on parenthood, Noah was his son. No one could take that away from him.

But what if Steph's family wanted to try? He assured himself they wouldn't have contacted the hospital. That didn't make sense. None of it made sense, but Ryder would figure it out. He glanced into the rearview mirror and took a deep breath.

Noah had drifted off to sleep, which he often did in the car, blissfully unaware that his daddy was having a slight panic attack in the front seat.

Ryder stiffened his jaw. He would protect his son no matter what this impromptu meeting threw his way. He might not be confident in his skills as a parent, but he would do anything for his child.

Esme stared out the window in the empty conference room next to the administrator's office at County Hospital, hoping the view of the outside world would calm her nerves.

As a kid, she'd been a shy bookworm and often escaped to the woods behind her family's two-story house to sit under her favorite tree and read for hours. Making real-life friends hadn't come easily to her as it had for her effervescent sister, so Anne Shirley, Hermione Granger and a host of other fictional characters became her beloved companions.

Today, the winter sky was a vivid blue, and a light breeze made the few leaves clinging to the branches of the trees along the edge of the parking lot flutter like a moth's wings. Sunlight shone brightly, a beacon from above that was in direct contrast to Esme's gray and turbulent mood.

After this meeting, she'd take Chase for a walk on the path bordering Lake Chatelaine to the west of downtown. Although she wasn't much for water sports, she loved being near the lake and watching birds dive toward the tiny bubbles that floated on the surface when the resident fish popped up.

"What is taking so long?" she asked her son, who sat in his infant carrier next to the table. Chase gurgled an answer before shoving one fist back in his mouth.

Maybe she should have called first, the way she'd planned, but after waking on the floor of the nursery with a kinked neck and aching back, Esme had decided the best way to gauge the response to her unthinkable suggestion would be to ask the question about the night Chase was born in person.

When Esme first arrived, the hospital's chief executive, Mary Dill, a woman who had to be nearing retirement age with a short pixie cut and round glasses that made her look like a blinking owl behind them, had appeared as shocked as Esme felt explaining the situation.

But Mary quickly converted to cover-your-assets mode, ushering Esme into the conference room to wait while she looked into the matter.

The matter, Esme had reminded the woman, was a human life—her baby. Chase was not simply a potential PR nightmare for the hospital to brush under a rug. The administrator had agreed and promised to handle her inquiries with the delicacy the situation warranted.

That was nearly forty minutes ago, Esme realized as she glanced at her watch. She stood, ready to track down some answers, but took her seat again when the door opened.

Mary entered, her skin noticeably paler than when Esme had interrupted her mid-bite of a breakfast sandwich. She was followed by a stuffy-looking man with shifty eyes and a paunch that seemed out of place on his wiry frame.

"Mrs. Fortune, this is Greg Oachs, hospital counsel."

"It's Miss, not Mrs.," Esme corrected as she shook the lawyer's outstretched hand. His grasp had all the enthusiasm of a stunned fish. "You can call me Esme."

"Then please call me Greg," he answered in a booming voice that seemed forcibly cheerful. "I understand we have a bit of a conundrum, Esme, but I assure you we'll get to the bottom of it. You can trust me on that."

She didn't trust anyone who made that claim but couldn't meet her gaze. Instead, the fine hairs on the back of her neck stood on end. Something was very wrong.

"Have you determined why my baby's DNA report came back the way it did?"

"We have an idea," Mary began before the lawyer cut her off with a sharp flick of the wrist.

"Let's wait until the other party arrives," he said in a commanding tone.

Normally, Esme would defer to someone in a position of authority, but Chase yawned at that moment, melting her heart and reminding her that there was someone more important than the attorney in this room. Her son mattered more than anyone or anything.

"I'm through waiting," she huffed, rising from her seat. "I expect answers to the questions I raised."

"She's not the only one," a deep voice said.

All three turned as a man in a well-cut suit entered the room. Esme would have pegged him for another attorney, except he had one arm looped around the handle of an infant carrier and sported a somewhat desperate glint in his piercing green eyes that convinced her he was the father of the baby he carried.

He looked to be around Esme's age, tall with sandy blond hair, broad shoulders and a chiseled jaw. The man possessed a kind of movie-star attractiveness that seemed out of place in this nondescript conference room.

As the stranger stepped closer, and his green eyes met hers, a memory tugged at the corner of Esme's mind. The realization dawned that she was staring at the big oaf from the night of her labor and delivery.

"You must be Ryder," Mary Dill said, thrusting out her hand with more enthusiasm than she'd displayed when Esme had appeared asking questions. "Thank you so much for coming in on such short notice."

"I didn't feel like I had a choice, given the ambiguity of your phone call." He briefly shook her hand and then glanced toward the other man in attendance. "You must be the lawyer."

"Greg Oachs of Oachs, Hart and Meinig. I'm general counsel for County Hospital."

"General counsel." Ryder frowned and placed the infant carrier on the conference table like it was the most natural thing in the world. "That sounds serious." His gaze tracked to Esme. "Do you know what this is about?" he asked as if somehow understanding they were on the same side, although he clearly didn't remember their brief eye-contact connection three months earlier.

"Not a clue," she said quietly.

"I can explain," Mary told them, although she looked like she might rather stick a fork in her eye.

"*I'll* explain." Greg placed his hands on the table and leaned forward before glancing at Ryder. "Would you like to put that thing on the floor?" He gestured toward the infant carrier.

"My *son*?" Ryder shook his head and placed a protective hand on the baby, making Esme's heart flutter. "No. He's fine right where he is."

Chase wasn't fine. He'd started to fuss a bit. She undid the harness and picked him up from the carrier, cradling the boy in her arms.

"About three months?" Ryder asked, his tone gentler than when he'd spoken to the attorney.

"Yes."

"Mine, too."

Should she tell him they'd been in the hospital on

the same fateful night? Esme wondered where his baby's mother was, hoping the woman had managed to overcome her insistence that she wasn't meant to be a mom.

Before she could say anything, Greg Oachs cleared his throat. "These two babies were born on the same night."

"You both remember?" Mary asked hopefully.

Greg sent the administrator a quelling glance, and Esme nearly scoffed. Of course, she remembered the night her son was born.

"Why are we here?" Ryder demanded, clearly not in the mood to walk down memory lane with a trio of strangers. "Is someone threatening to sue the hospital over the conditions we dealt with the night of the storm?"

"We did our best," the hospital administrator insisted.

"No one is filing suit." Greg straightened and tugged at his tie, leaving it crooked against his white oxford-cloth shirt. "There was a misunderstanding back in October." His throat bobbed as he swallowed and looked at a place past Esme's shoulder. "We have reason to believe your babies were accidentally switched shortly after they were born."

Esme had been expecting the words, but they still hit with the force of a mallet cracking the side of her skull. She drew Chase closer to her chest, sending a silent prayer that this was a nightmare she'd soon wake from.

Ryder stood in stunned silence for several seconds, then dropped into a chair like his legs wouldn't hold him.

She understood the feeling. Her entire body had gone numb, except her heart, which burned as if the words were a hot poker stabbing into it.

"What makes you think that?" Ryder demanded finally.

"Chase and I had testing done," she told him before the attorney or administrator could spin the story. "My ex-husband was in an accident and died suddenly. I wanted to know more about his side of the family." In truth, she hadn't considered learning more about Seth's family history until Freya gifted her the two test kits.

Ryder inclined his head. "I'm sorry for your loss."

"My *son*'s loss," she clarified, unsure why she needed to make that distinction. "His results came back with no one from either side of the family listed, as if we don't share DNA."

"Could it have been a mistake at the testing facility?"

The attorney cleared his throat again. "I think—"

"I didn't ask what you thought," Ryder snapped. "We'll get to you in a minute."

Greg Oachs crossed his arms over his chest with an audible harrumph but said nothing more.

"I apologize." Ryder returned his gaze to Esme. "I also didn't catch your name."

"Esme Fortune," she told him. "I spoke with someone at 411 Me last night. They assured me Chase's results are valid."

"We'd like you and your son to take a DNA test," Mary said to Ryder, then transferred her gaze to Esme. "You and your baby as well."

"I've already done that," she answered.

"For our purposes," the woman explained. "We'd like to have both of your test results on file here at the hospital."

"Okay," Esme murmured.

"You don't have to agree to anything," Ryder said, his deep gaze intense on hers.

"I have to know." She dropped a kiss on the top of Chase's downy head. "Don't you want to know?"

"I want to go back to bed, wake up and pretend this day never happened."

She smiled slightly. "If only that were an option."

"It is," Greg offered with more of that fake cheer. "Or you can take the tests, and if the results come back the way we think they might, it's an easy swap. No harm, no foul."

Even Mary Dill gasped at that suggestion.

Esme felt like she'd taken another blow, this one directly to her heart. Chase was her child, the baby she'd brought home from the hospital. Her son. How could she conceive of any other possibility?

"You're going to want to stop talking," Ryder told the attorney. "Because everything coming out of your mouth makes me want to slam my fist into it."

"Th-there's no need to get violent," Greg stammered, taking a step away from the table.

"You have no idea what I need," Ryder muttered.

"I need to get out of here," Esme blurted, then

looked at Mary. "Can we do the tests right now? I want to go home."

"Of course," she answered without hesitation.

Esme kept Chase cradled close in one arm and picked up the infant carrier with her free hand.

"We'll put a rush on the tests," Mary said as Esme moved around the conference table. Sunlight streamed through the windows she'd been staring out earlier, and the brightness of the day felt like it was mocking her. "But it will be later today until we have the results."

The attorney reached for his briefcase. "I have some papers for you both to sign granting the hospital indemnity in this matter."

"Neither of us is signing a damn thing," Ryder answered for them both, which was fine. Esme didn't have any fight left in her at the moment. This new version of her reality was too much to manage.

She was surprised when Ryder followed her and Mary out of the room, gripping his son's infant carrier with the same tight hold she had on Chase's.

"Are you willing to have the tests?" she asked, then glanced at the sweet baby sleeping in the carrier. "What's his name?"

"Noah," Ryder whispered, then touched her arm. "I understand we're strangers, Esme Fortune, but as far as I'm concerned, we're in this together."

She nodded, his unexpected words comforting her, much like his gaze had the night their babies were born. Once again, she needed all the reassurance she could get.

Chapter Three

A half hour later, Esme stood outside the hospital's entrance and dialed her sister's number with shaking fingers. Bea answered on the first ring, and she quickly explained the situation, even the awful part where the attorney suggested they swap babies.

Bea was outraged but also shocked at how calm Esme sounded. It wasn't calm—she couldn't feel anything. Her body—her entire being—had gone numb because the alternative of feeling fear, panic and dread about the potential outcome of this situation was too much to cope with at the moment.

"Who are the parents of the other baby?" Her sister's voice was low like she hated even asking about them.

"I only met the father." Esme realized she hadn't thought to ask about the absence of Noah's mother from the meeting. Chalk it up to one more unanswered question. "His name is Ryder Hayes, and he—"

"Oh, no," her sister murmured. "Stay away from anyone in Chatelaine with the last name Hayes. I'm serious, Esme."

"How can I do that, Bea? What's wrong with Ryder Hayes?" Esme glanced down at the infant carrier that held her son, which she'd placed on a bench in the shade while she called her sister and regrouped. Chase was sleeping peacefully, his rosebud mouth working like he was having a delightful dream. If only Ryder's wish for a do-over on this nightmare of a morning could come true.

"There are two brothers, but I don't know which is Ryder. One seems more reserved, but the other is a total player. They work for their dad, who bought the LC Club with plans to make it even fancier than it is already. The father acts like he owns the whole world, and the rest of us are lucky to breathe the same air as him."

Esme's least favorite type of person. She was familiar with the exclusive gated community and private club situated on the banks of Lake Chatelaine, although she'd never stepped foot in the place. Swanky social clubs weren't exactly her style, but she could see the handsome man with the expensive suit and vibrant eyes fitting in there.

"I don't have the choice to ignore him," she told her sister. "We're in this together." Repeating the words Ryder had spoken made her heart catch. Had he meant that, or had he been feeding her a line to soften her defenses so he could manipulate her?

Before she'd been caught in the spell of her late husband's magnetic personality and the lies he'd told, Esme had believed she possessed a strong sense for reading people. But she'd been so wrong about Seth. His subtle digs at her confidence and discovering after his death that he'd been cheating on her almost from the time of their first date caused her to doubt everything—especially herself.

"Okay, but I'm warning you to be careful. You can't trust Ryder Hayes."

A slight shiver passed through Esme, and she turned to see the man in question exiting the hospital. Her and Chase's tests had been completed first, and she'd slipped out of the hospital lab after they were finished. She'd heard Ryder in the next room demanding that Mary Dill give him a list of everyone on staff during the shift when Chase and Noah were born.

All she'd wanted was to get out of the building. What she longed to do was run and ignore everything, but something had stopped her from driving away.

Ryder stood outside the sliding doors, unaware of her presence. He held the handle of the infant carrier in both hands, and his head dropped forward, shoulders slumping like they carried an unbearable weight.

"I've got to go, Bea," she said into the phone. "I'll call you later."

"I'm here for whatever you need. We'll get you and Chase through this, Es."

She said goodbye, disconnected and placed her phone in one of the pockets of the diaper bag she always carried. As much as Esme appreciated her sister's support, Bea couldn't possibly understand the impact those routine test results were having on Esme's future.

No one did, except perhaps Ryder Hayes. But still, she couldn't afford to be naive about the situation. Maybe Bea was right, and he couldn't be trusted and was a womanizer like Seth. Was that why his wife or girlfriend hadn't come with him today? She hated to think about her son being exposed to that kind of a role model.

But it wasn't only Chase she needed to worry about. Noah was a part of the equation that couldn't be ignored.

As the numbness wore off, a tumble of tumultuous emotions threatened to drown her. Of all the things Esme wanted right now, first and foremost, she did *not* want to be alone.

She picked up Chase's car seat and walked in Ryder's direction. He continued to stand like a statue, seemingly unaware of anything around him.

"Hello?" She stopped a few feet away, and the panic in his gaze when he glanced up at her felt like a direct hit to her heart.

Then his eyes cleared, and he offered her a weak smile. "I'm trying not to freak out."

"How's that going?"

He chuckled weakly. "Not well."

Ryder's phone vibrated from inside his suit coat pocket, and he absently patted the device but didn't answer the call.

"I heard that thing go off several times during the meeting." She tucked a lock of hair behind her ear, noticing that his gaze tracked her movement. "It sounds like someone is desperate to get a hold of you." Was it Noah's mother? She wanted to ask.

"I missed an important work meeting this morning." His throat bobbed as he swallowed. "Quite possibly wrecked my career because of it. Somehow that doesn't seem to matter."

Those weren't the words of a manipulative, power-hungry man as far as Esme was concerned. Seth's smarmy behavior might have shaken her faith in her instincts, but she believed Ryder was as disturbed by all of this as her. Either that, or he'd missed his calling as an actor.

For the first time since discovering how badly her late husband had betrayed her, she wanted to trust someone again, even though the man in question was almost a stranger. A stranger with whom she shared an unimaginable connection.

"What are we going to do?" He searched her face as if he believed she'd have an answer.

Apparently, Ryder Hayes trusted Esme with a confidence she hadn't granted herself in a long time, and she wanted to live up to his expectations. She needed to prove—mostly to herself—that she was strong and capable. Her son was going to need her to be just that.

"I'm not sure," she answered because there was no denying that truth. "But I know we'll figure it out. We both want what's best for our babies." She cleared her throat and then offered the most genuine smile she could muster under the circumstances. "Would you like to come back to my house while we wait for the results? We could talk and..."

He offered a small smile. "Yes, we could talk."

She shrugged. "I guess we should get to know each other, given how our lives are about to be intertwined."

"Intertwined," Ryder repeated like he was testing the word to see how it felt on his tongue. "Yes, I'd like to get to know you." He flashed a grin before glancing at Noah's infant carrier and then Chase's. "I'd like to get to know you both."

Awareness skittered along her nerve endings, which was silly because the only connection she and Ryder had was the unfathomable situation they were facing together. This was not the time for her lady parts to wake up from their long slumber.

"I'm parked in the second row." She gestured to the half-full lot. "My address is 432 Maple. Easy enough if we get separated."

Ryder nodded and placed a hand on his jacket as the phone continued to vibrate. "We won't. I'll see you in a few minutes, Esme."

She liked the way her name sounded when he said it. That was *not* good. As Esme secured Chase's car seat in the base, she reminded herself that she had approximately ten minutes to kill the fluttery feelings that flitted through her stomach unbidden each time Ryder's green eyes caught on hers.

This was business—the business of taking care of her baby. It would never be anything more.

Before climbing out of his BMW sedan in front of Esme's house with Noah's baby carrier in tow, Ryder switched his phone from vibrate to full-on "do not disturb" mode. He'd made the mistake of glancing at it on the way over. The multiple voice mails he'd received from his brother and the half dozen texts his father had sent demanding that Ryder get his ass to the office sooner than later were a reality check he did not want or need. This latest development in his complicated life would make things even more challenging.

He wasn't sure when it had become an unquestionable fact within their family that he and Brandon, thirteen months younger than Ryder, would be expected to compete in every aspect of their lives.

Dear old Dad loved a good challenge, never shying away from a chance to battle for a top spot, and Brandon was happy to emulate him. Although he did his best to hide it, Ryder took after their mother in ways that would send his father into an apoplectic fit if he realized the extent of it. He had learned early on to tamp down his sensitive nature, and by the time he was ten, the fleshy part of his palms had deeply worn grooves from where he dug his nails whenever he'd had the urge to cry or show weakness in front of his dad and brother.

Chandler Hayes pitted his sons against one another in everything from backyard games of tag and shooting hoops to grades, girls and football. Ryder had done his best to deflect the expectations without making his father think he was a wimp, which, according to Chandler, was the worst thing a boy could be.

He'd tried just enough in school not to draw attention, avoided dating altogether and opted to play tight end instead of quarterback so he wouldn't have to compete with Brandon for the marquee spot on their high-school team at the private school they'd attended in one of Houston's poshest neighborhoods.

It wasn't that Ryder didn't believe he deserved a chance to shine or that he couldn't beat his brother when push came to shove, which it often had in the backyard. He just hadn't wanted to put his energy into fighting and instead liked to lead a team by example and earn a grade or an award on his own merit, not motivated by some false sense of resentment toward his brother.

But the CEO position his father was vacating at the end of the month was a different story. Ryder had the talent, commitment and vision to lead Hayes Enterprises into the future, and he wanted to create a legacy to leave for his son, only not at the expense of being a father who was present in a meaningful way.

Ryder had dealt with that reality his entire life, and it wasn't worth the price he or Noah would pay.

He drew in a deep breath as he approached the front porch of the compact brick house painted a cheery yellow. Black shutters framed the front window, and the rocking chair on the porch sported a pillow with a heart embroidered on it that matched the heart-shaped wreath hanging on the door.

Valentine's Day. The holiday for people who believed in love was fast approaching, not that it would make a difference in Ryder's solitary life. Maybe he'd order Noah one of those "heartbreaker" onesies he'd seen online.

Esme had mentioned her husband dying in an unexpected accident, which was another thing they had in common. Unlike Ryder and Stephanie, had she and her late husband been blissfully in love?

Although their relationship had been fraught with drama, Ryder's chest still tightened each time he thought about the fact that his son would grow up without a mother.

When the door opened and Esme stood smiling at him from the other side, the vise that held his chest in its grip loosened considerably. He wished he could explain what it was about his unexpected partner in this dramatic turn of events that had such a calming effect on his nerves.

Esme was pretty in a girl-next-door kind of way. She had shiny dark-chocolate-colored hair that fell just below her shoulders and the clearest green eyes he'd ever seen. As he stared into them now, he noticed they'd taken on a gray hue, like the waves the wind whipped up across Lake Chatelaine, which he could see from the apartment he'd rented near the LC Club on the other side of town.

As far as Ryder could tell, she wasn't wearing makeup, and other than tiny gold hoops in her ears, she sported no jewelry. He dated women with more outward flash and pizzazz because they seemed to be the type who didn't expect more from him than an expensive dinner and a mutually pleasurable roll in the sheets.

Esme was the type of woman a man would bring home to meet his family, although he didn't consider that an option with his dad and brother. The last girl he'd introduced to his family had been someone he'd brought home over fall break during his sophomore year of college.

He'd liked her quite a bit, but the very next weekend, his brother had taken that same girl to a fraternity formal. Always a competition between the two of them, at least from Brandon's viewpoint.

Ryder couldn't put his finger on what had made him suddenly so consumed with ruminating on the past. He typically kept his gaze forward because looking back didn't do a damn bit of good.

He blinked when he realized Esme was snapping her fingers in front of his face.

"I asked whether you wanted to come in or if you planned to stand on the porch all day?" She scrunched up her nose in a rather adorable way. "I can bring you a glass of water if you'd like."

He scrubbed a hand over his jaw. "Sorry. I'd love

to come in. It feels like my head is spinning in a million different directions."

"Mine, too," she admitted as he walked past her into the cozy living room.

There was an overstuffed couch on one wall with a leather chair and ottoman and a coffee table that looked like it might have been up-cycled from wood pallets. A basic TV sat on an entertainment center with framed photos on either side, including several of Esme's baby, Chase.

Glancing down at his son, it made him realize that although he'd taken loads of photos of Noah and texted them regularly to his mother back in Houston, he hadn't thought to have any printed and framed for display. His apartment held none of the homey touches like the colorful throw pillows and the fuzzy blanket draped across the back of the chair that made Esme's small house feel so warm and inviting.

"Do you sing lullabies to Chase?"

She looked surprised by the random question but nodded. "At some point, he's going to realize his mother can't carry a tune, but so far, I haven't made him cry outright with my singing."

"I don't know the words to any kids' songs." He placed the infant carrier on the sofa, Noah snuggled inside it and dozing peacefully. Ryder wished he felt any sense of that peace. "It probably seems like a minor detail, but I feel like somebody gave out parenting manuals, and I missed that day of class. I sing Bruce Springsteen songs just like my dad did when I was a baby."

As if he'd heard his father's words and wanted to make a request, Noah began to fuss.

"There aren't any manuals, and I don't think you can go wrong with The Boss." Esme bent down to trace a finger over Noah's soft cheek. "Would it be okay with you if I held him?"

"I'm sure he'd love someone more capable than me giving him a cuddle," Ryder said with a laugh, immediately realizing his lame attempt at humor had fallen flat based on the incredulous look she gave him.

"I'm sure he loves his daddy," she assured him, then turned her attention to Noah. "Is your daddy the best?" she asked in a tone so gentle it made Ryder's knees turn to mush. Noah responded with a few plaintive cries but quickly settled into Esme's arms.

She kept her gaze on the baby for a few seconds, but when she looked up at Ryder again, her eyes were filled with tears.

"What's wrong?" His heart began to hammer in his chest. He might not know Esme well, but the last thing he wanted was to see her cry.

She shook her head. "He looks like my brother and I did in baby photos," she whispered. "I'm sure that sounds—"

The sound of crying crackling through the monitor on the coffee table drowned out her words.

"I put Chase down in his crib when we got home, but I didn't swaddle him. He doesn't go down as well on his own." She started for the stairs and then seemed to realize she was already holding a baby.

"I'll get him if that's okay," Ryder offered.

"First door on your left at the top of the stairs."

Mind reeling all over again in response to Esme's claim that Noah resembled her as a baby, he sprinted up the steps and let himself into the lavender-scented nursery.

Chase, who seemed to be a bit further along with his ability to self-soothe than Noah, was happily sucking on his fist when Ryder peered over the side of the crib.

The baby's arms and legs began flailing in excitement as he spotted Ryder, who smiled as he scooped up the boy. His smile faded as a realization pounded through him.

Chase Fortune looked like a Hayes, right down to the cleft in his chin. Ryder locked his legs and closed his eyes as emotion pushed him to the edge of his control. Then he leaned down and kissed the head of the child he knew without a doubt to be his biological son.

Chapter Four

"If my great-aunt hadn't gifted me the 411 Me testing, I don't know when or if I would have realized the switch occurred." Esme stared at the paperwork on the empty sofa cushion between her and Ryder. If only her house had a fireplace, she could burn the report that had changed her life.

Not that destroying it would do any good now. They knew the truth, and there was no going back. In a way, she owed even more of a debt to Freya Fortune. It would have been horrible to discover what had happened that night at the hospital years from now. She and Ryder would have missed so many milestones with their sons.

"I can accept the facts," she said, placing a gentle kiss on Chase's forehead. "But I don't know how I'm supposed to stop loving one baby because I now have room in my heart for both of them."

"Noah's test results haven't come back yet," Ryder reminded her, then shook his head. "Sorry. That's a stupid thing to say. We don't need tests to confirm what we know in our hearts."

He looked down at Noah, who was sleeping in his strong arms. "I'm still having trouble accepting any of this, especially when the hospital doesn't seem to have answers."

As soon as Ryder came down the stairs holding Chase, he'd insisted on calling Mary Dill at the hospital with another request for a list of the staff working the night Chase and Noah were born. It was obvious the lawyer had coached the hospital administrator on what to say because she'd been unwilling to divulge any information, citing privacy laws and making excuses about bureaucratic red tape.

Ryder's frustration had been palpable, and both babies fussed in response to the tension filling Esme's living room. She shared his exasperation but knew they had to stay calm and work together for the best interest of both of their sons.

She'd pulled out a notepad and the 411 Me report so they could regroup and make a plan of action while they waited for the official results from the lab.

"You're amazing," Ryder said out of the blue, and Esme did a double take, finding it hard to believe he was directing the compliment toward her.

She squirmed under the weight of his impassioned stare. "I haven't done anything."

"Yes, you have. You're keeping me from losing it," he answered with a laugh. "I can tell Noah is also responding to your steady presence." Ryder checked his watch. "He typically has a meltdown around this time of day. Even his babysitter has commented on how she can set a watch by his crying."

"I'm happy to help, although I'm not sure I deserve much credit." Esme shrugged. "Chase has his days and nights mixed up, so it's party time here in the wee hours."

He grinned. "I never realized how much I took a full night's sleep for granted."

"Can I ask you a question? It might be too personal, but—"

"Anything," he interrupted. "You can ask me anything."

"It's about Noah's…" She paused and swallowed around the emotion that bubbled up in her throat. Esme *was* Noah's biological mother. They were waiting for confirmation from the hospital, yet the truth of her connection to Ryder's baby was written on her heart. "Where is your wife or girlfriend in all of this? Doesn't she—"

"Stephanie died in a car wreck when Noah was a month old." Ryder closed his eyes for a moment and drew in a shuddery breath.

"I'm so sorry."

He nodded and focused on her again, his green eyes now the color of a dark evergreen tree. "Can I tell you something I haven't shared with anyone?"

"Yes," she whispered.

"Steph was on her way from Chatelaine to San Antonio when the accident happened. Things had not been going well between us. She'd gotten pregnant less than a month after we started dating and was nearly six months along before she realized it." He shook his head. "She thought she had a chronic case of indigestion."

Esme had heard of circumstances where a woman remained unaware of the baby growing inside her but found it difficult to fathom. She'd felt the difference in her body almost immediately.

"We were no longer together when she found out she was pregnant," Ryder continued, "but she wanted to have the baby so we decided to try again for the child's sake. I proposed marriage, but Steph refused. That should have been a sign. There were so many signs, but I figured they could be chalked up to nerves. Things got worse after Noah was born."

"Worse, how?" Esme asked, almost dreading the answer.

"She didn't like being a mother. We talked to the doctor, and I suggested she see a therapist. I thought maybe she was dealing with postpartum depression and tried to support her. But I couldn't do it in the way she needed. My job is demanding…"

"Yeah, I got that impression based on how your phone vibrated nonstop," she murmured.

He sighed. "I should have taken more time off, but my dad had just moved the company headquarters to Chatelaine and announced his impending retirement. I travel a lot in my current role, so earning a promotion that would allow me to stay close to home felt essential for Noah."

Ryder tightened his hold on the baby, and it was obvious that he felt the strain of balancing work with fatherhood. "Steph didn't like being a full-time caregiver. We had a fight the night she left, and she packed a bag and headed out the door, telling me she wouldn't be back."

Esme gasped, then reached for his free hand at the look of guilt that flashed in his gaze. "You couldn't have known what would happen."

"No," he agreed hoarsely. "But that doesn't stop me from blaming myself. My son doesn't have a mother, and maybe if I'd taken a true leave of absence or changed more diapers—"

"You can't do that." Esme squeezed his large hand, noting the calluses inside his palm. She wouldn't have expected work-roughened skin from a man who appeared so polished and professional. "Neither of us can be blamed for the circumstances that brought us here."

He didn't look convinced.

"Ryder, I carried a baby inside me for nine months, and I loved my son from the moment I learned about him. I'm sorry it wasn't the same for your Stephanie."

"You're nothing like her," Ryder said quietly. The conviction in his voice assured Esme he was offering her a compliment, but she didn't take a chance on asking.

Based on the tidbits of information her sister had shared about the Hayes men and their family's reputation, she wasn't anywhere near the type of woman Ryder would consider a romantic partner. But that wasn't what was important at this moment.

"I gave birth to a baby I thought I knew. As a mother, I would have told you I'd recognize my child anywhere and under any circumstance. Now it's just as clear that you are holding the baby I gave birth to. How do you think it makes me feel?" It was his turn to squeeze her hand; the warmth of his skin seeped into her body, grounding her with his solid touch.

"I imagine it makes you angry, confused and like you want to understand how this could have happened as much as I do."

If only it were that simple. "It makes me feel like I failed as a mother from the very start. Not only my son but yours as well."

She tugged her hand out of his and dashed it across her cheeks. Tears would do no good, but she couldn't stop them. She looked down at the boy in her arms, unwilling to meet Ryder's gaze and the censure she expected to see there. Of course, he hadn't recognized her negligence as a mother at the start of all this. The shock had precluded every other rational thought. But now that she'd pointed it out, how could he help but agree?

If she'd noticed the mistake—whether done unintentionally or…well…she couldn't imagine someone would have caused this chaos on purpose. But she should have seen it. She was a *mother*. She should have known.

She didn't look up as she heard Ryder rise from

the couch. Was he going to walk out on her the way Seth had? Could she blame him? A moment later, his weight settled next to her, and his arm came around her shoulder in a tender embrace.

"You can't be kind to me right now," she said, her voice shaking. "That's really going to start the waterworks, and I know from experience that men don't like waterworks."

She felt more than heard the laugh reverberate in his chest. "I never want to make a woman cry, but I'm not afraid of your tears, Esme. There are plenty of things that scare the hell out of me, and being a good father tops that list. But you can cry all you need to, sweetheart. It's fine by me, and I can guaran-damn-tee you that we're not going to raise our boys to be put off by emotions. I've been there—done that. I don't recommend it."

Esme wiped a tear off of Chase's forehead, then transferred her gaze to Noah, who was still sleeping soundly in the crook of Ryder's arm. Finally, she looked up at the man who'd become her closest—if unlikely—ally in this mess of a situation.

A sudden idea flashed across her mind like a lightning bolt from that October storm. Goose bumps erupted along her skin and then disappeared just as quickly as the notion settled with the weight of a boulder in the middle of the road that would not be ignored.

"What is it?" Ryder asked softly. His green eyes darkened as he leaned in closer. For a brief moment, she thought he might be about to kiss her.

"I think we should raise our sons together."

His head snapped back, and whatever potential moment had been about to occur was forgotten. Maybe it had only been a figment of Esme's too vivid imagination.

"How would that work?" His thick brows drew together. "Are you proposing—"

"A partnership. Platonic, of course," she amended quickly, knowing he'd never agree to anything more. Not that she wanted more. Her focus was doing what was best for Chase and Noah.

Liar, her body whispered, and Esme patently ignored it.

"A partnership," Ryder echoed. "We'd raise the boys like we were both their parents?"

Color rose to her cheeks. "It probably sounds outlandish, but that's how my dad was raised."

"Your dad was switched at birth?"

She shook her head, trying to make sense of her muddled thoughts, which was difficult with Ryder so close. "No, it was a different circumstance. My grandfather, Edgar Fortune, and his brother, Elias, were not the most upstanding men or fathers. The family rumor is that they were on the run after an accident here in Chatelaine at the mine they owned with their brothers."

"I heard about that tragedy," Ryder said with a nod. "There's a plaque hanging in the foyer of the LC Club commemorating the fifty men who died when the silver mine collapsed. However, there's no mention of a connection to the Fortunes."

"They were chased out of town—or took off on their own, depending on who you ask—pretty quickly after pinning responsibility on the mining foreman. Edgar and Elias spent some time in Cave Creek and met my grandma and great-aunt. But they didn't stick around there either, even after learning they were going to be fathers. So the jilted girlfriends decided to raise their babies together. My dad and his cousin grew up as close as brothers. Neither of them knew their fathers, but the family my grandma and great-aunt created was something for them."

He continued to stare at her, so she went on, "My sister and brother and I weren't close with our cousins growing up, but that could change now that we're all here. I moved to town because my great-uncle's widow—her name is Freya Fortune—is using part of the inheritance Uncle Elias left her to help out his three grandchildren and my brother, sister and me. She wants to transform the reputation of our branch of the Fortunes in Chatelaine. She's helping each of us fulfill our dearest wish."

"That's amazing," Ryder murmured. "It must have come as quite a surprise."

"It did. My older sister, Bea, has been a waitress forever, but now she's going to open her own restaurant. And Asa, my big brother, came to town last summer and fell in love with a dude ranch he hopes to buy. They're going to make a difference in this community."

"What's your wish, Esme?" Ryder's voice felt like a caress against her skin, and she had a hard time remembering her own name, let alone how Freya was helping her.

She winced as the answer came to her. "This is going to sound silly compared to what my siblings plan to do, but I was already pregnant when Freya contacted us. Ever since the first test came back positive, my wish has been to be a good mother to my baby."

Gesturing to the room around them, she continued, "I was able to buy this house with my late husband's life insurance policy payout, and Freya has given me an amount that matches what I'd make as a teacher for the school year. She also gave me an open account at GreatStore to buy whatever I need for Chase."

"You're a teacher?" he asked, his mouth curving at one end. "That suits you."

"Thanks, I think." She bit down on her lower lip. "I'll go back to work next year, but I adore being with Chase for now." She smiled down at her baby, certain this was the right thing to do. "I'd love to be able to take care of Noah as well. I'm sure your babysitter is great, but I can give them a mother's love. I want to be a mother to *both* of our sons."

When Ryder's eyes widened, Esme wondered if she'd said too much. This wasn't one of her beloved stories with a guaranteed happy ending. If Ryder decided he didn't want her in his son's life…where would that leave her? Chase might not be her biological child, but her heart didn't care, and it immediately expanded to include Noah.

She didn't have the charm that Asa did or the drive Bea possessed in wanting to make her dreams come true. All Esme had ever wanted was a happy life with a family who belonged to her.

Before the plane crash took their lives, her parents had lived more like bickering roommates than a couple who treasured growing old together. She knew they'd started as high school sweethearts, but by the time Esme had any concrete memories of their marriage, that bloom of first love had all but disappeared.

Her aunt and uncle hadn't been happy either, and with her grandfather's history, she wondered if it were possible that there could be some kind of missing piece in her branch of the Fortune family tree that would prevent her from being happy.

Esme had hoped to find true love, but after Seth's betrayal, she couldn't imagine opening her heart again and being hurt by a man. Maybe she simply wasn't worthy of being loved and carried the black mark of the unhappy couples who came before her. But she liked Ryder, and her gut told her he was a good man. He would be a great father, and really, what more could she ask for?

"My son," Ryder said slowly, then cleared his throat. "Both of our sons would be lucky to have you as a mother. I might not know what I'm doing as a parent, but I'm not a fool." He nodded. "Raising them together is the right decision. We're a team, Esme."

She released the breath lodged in her lungs and smiled. "We're going to make this work," she assured him. "It will be okay because Chase and Noah will remain our top priorities." She waved a hand. "Not that I'm going to place expectations on you like that you can't date or whatever. I'm sure you—"

"The last thing on my mind is dating," Ryder said, then seemed uncomfortable at what his comment might insinuate about Esme and glanced at his watch. "I should check in at the office. It's nearly the end of the business day, and I'm guessing we won't hear from the hospital until tomorrow."

She tried not to be disappointed. She hadn't been referring to the two of them dating, anyway, so had no reason for the pang in her chest. Besides, if Ryder was the player her sister seemed to believe, he'd show his true colors soon enough. Nothing else mattered as long as he followed the rules they established and was a kind and loving father to the two boys.

"We'll need rules," she announced.

One of his thick brows raised in response. "For the record, I'm better at making rules than following them."

"We'll make them together after we get confirmation from the hospital," she clarified. "I know what the tests are going to reveal, but we should hear it from them just the same."

"Fine," Ryder agreed. "And if they don't give us information on the nurses and doctors who staffed the labor and delivery unit that night, then we'll track down those individuals on our own."

There was a confidence in his tone she hadn't heard before, and for the first time, Esme understood that Ryder Hayes was not a man used to compromise or making concessions.

"Do you want me to keep Noah here while you go to your office? I'm happy to watch both of them during the week while you're at work. I don't have much of a life outside of being a mom."

Ugh. Why had she shared that with him? It only made her sound even more pathetic. Like she had no aspirations beyond being a mother and nothing to occupy her time but babies.

She had to be the most boring woman Ryder had ever met.

"I'd appreciate that." He stood, then frowned as a loud gurgle followed by a foul stench came from the vicinity of Noah's diaper. "I can change him first."

"Leave him to me," she said and shifted Chase's weight to one arm so she could cradle Noah with the other. "Go be corporate and important and all that," she told Ryder, who looked both grateful and incredulous. "We'll be here when you get home."

Home. What an odd concept to share with a virtual stranger, but the word felt appropriate. She believed in her heart this was right.

Chapter Five

As Ryder walked through the Hayes Enterprises of-
fices on the LC Club's first floor, a hush fell over the
open-concept office space. No one, from the recep-
tionist in the lobby to the sales team to the account-
ing and HR staff, would make eye contact with him.

The silence felt like a judgment, and he began singing what he considered Noah's favorite Bruce Springsteen song in his head to distract himself from the
dread he felt. Esme had told him he couldn't go wrong
with The Boss, but the gaping pit in his stomach widened on the way toward his father's corner office.

As he passed the conference room, his brother
walked out, briefcase in hand. Ryder wasn't sure if
Brandon kept supplies besides gum and hair gel in
that leather satchel. Because he didn't use it for anything other than holding it up to wave, as he did now.

"Bro, you missed a hell of a meeting," Brandon said. "I'm heading out to catch up with a few team members at the LC Club bar. Do you want to join us and congratulate me on how impressive I was?" His brother chucked him on the arm. "By *impressive*, I mean at least I had the good sense to attend a meeting with half the upper management staff and several key investors. I hope you had a good excuse this time, Ryder. Not like those bogus doctor's appointments."

Brandon emphasized the phrase *doctor's appointments* with air quotes, and Ryder silently counted to ten. "Noah's well visits aren't bogus." He forced a smile. "I'm glad things went smoothly. We all play for the same team. Remember, this isn't horse under the basketball hoop in the backyard. You're not trying to outshoot me. I want you to do well."

Brandon's mouth opened and closed a couple of times like he didn't know how to respond to Ryder not engaging in an argument. Arguing was typically the bulk of his relationship with his brother, but no matter how much he wanted the CEO position, Ryder was sick and tired of fighting.

The events of this day had put his priorities into sharp focus. The truth was that even though he hustled to be the best parent he could, he hadn't been doing enough, especially considering how effortless Esme made it look. Ryder would have ended up rocking in a corner if somebody had asked him to take care of two babies at once. Not that he could say any of that to his brother.

"Is Dad still in his office?"

"Don't tell me you're going to try to patch things up with him right now." Brandon narrowed his eyes. "It's not going to work. Give it a day or so. I doubt he's in the mood for your excuses, Ry."

Excuses. That was rich. "I need to talk to both of you," Ryder said. "It has to do with Noah. This is serious, Bran."

His brother's demeanor changed instantly. He shifted from smug victor to concerned uncle, and Ryder knew it was genuine. Even though Noah couldn't appreciate it yet, Brandon took his future role of a fun uncle, or "funcle" as he called himself, just as seriously as he took outdoing Ryder at every turn. "What's going on with Noah?"

Instead of answering, Ryder continued toward their dad's office, confident Brandon would follow. He waved off his father's assistant, opening the door after a cursory knock.

Chandler Hayes sat behind his massive mahogany desk, the same one Ryder and Brandon had played under as young boys. The custom piece had been ordered from Italy early in their father's career to commemorate Chandler's first million-dollar deal.

The ornate desk looked out of place in the LC Club building, which boasted a rustic vibe, but it represented something to Ryder's father, a reminder to everyone who walked in that Chandler Hayes was an important man.

Ryder recognized the look of dissatisfaction in

his dad's hard brown eyes. He'd seen it often enough over the years.

"I'm busy at the moment, Ryder," his father said, glancing down at the papers before him. "Just like you apparently were this morning. You should have answered my calls. Make an appointment with—"

"Noah was switched at birth with another baby." Ryder heard the soft click of the door shutting behind Brandon as his announcement was greeted with stunned silence.

"What are you talking about?" his father asked finally, pushing back from the desk, his fingers tightly gripping the edge.

"That was what kept me from being here earlier."

"It has to be a mistake," Brandon said, coming to stand next to Ryder. "Noah looks like a Hayes. He *is* a Hayes."

Somehow, the shock his brother and father displayed was a comfort to Ryder. The relationship the three of them shared often felt dysfunctional at its core, so he'd been unsure how the two of them would greet his news.

"We're waiting for his DNA test to come back—"

"Then you don't know for certain," Chandler interrupted.

"I *know*," Ryder answered definitively. "He and the other baby, born the same night, could be twins. But Chase has the Hayes cleft in his chin." Ryder rubbed a hand against his jaw. "And Noah looks like his biological mother."

"I don't understand…" his father muttered.

"Esme, the other baby's mother, had DNA testing done for her son—a gift from a family member. The results reported that she shared no DNA with her child, and members of our family showed up in his genetic profile. The hospital attorney called me this morning, and Noah and I went in for a meeting." He shook his head. "I don't need a test to confirm what I know in my heart to be true. I can't explain how the mistake happened, but we'll get to the bottom of it."

"We?" his father asked.

"Esme Fortune and me," Ryder clarified. Simply saying her name out loud calmed him. He wished he could bottle her soothing and sweet personality to call upon whenever he needed to talk to his dad or Brandon.

"Your new baby mama is a Fortune?" Brandon snorted. "Way to set a high bar."

"Don't call her that," Ryder snapped, his temper flaring. "Neither Esme nor I chose this, but we're going to work together to do what's best for our boys."

"I was joking," Brandon insisted, lifting his hands like he was ready to ward off a physical blow. "You're a good father, Ry. You'll do the right thing."

"Do we need to get the lawyers involved?" his father asked, already picking up the phone. Chandler Hayes was the only person Ryder knew who still preferred talking on a landline.

"No, Dad. It's fine for now." Ryder stepped toward the desk and then sat in one of the tufted leather chairs in front of it. "Though I appreciate the support."

He was both grateful and slightly shell-shocked. Offering to sic the company attorneys on someone was akin to a warm hug from his dad.

Chandler placed the receiver back on the cradle and frowned. "What do you know about this Fortune woman?"

"Not a lot yet, but my gut tells me to trust her. She's a good mother and wants to do the right thing." He drew a deep breath and continued, "So do I, which is why I'd like to take personal leave for the next two weeks."

Brandon let out a low whistle behind him and whispered, "Bro."

The one syllable was thick with meaning, but Ryder couldn't worry about that now.

"Why?" his father demanded.

"Because Noah and Chase need me to step up. That means being fully present during this transition. Esme and I are going to raise our sons together." His heart clenched at the thought of those two innocent babies thrust into this inconceivable situation. "Just because Noah isn't my biological child doesn't change the fact that I love him. I love Chase, too."

"The Fortune woman shares this sentiment?" Chandler raised a brow. "What about her husband?"

"Late husband," Ryder clarified. "And she's not after my money, Dad. Neither of us asked for this, but we're going to make it work." Saying the words solidified his conviction that they were doing the right thing. "I don't have a lot of answers, but you can bet I'm going to find them. I need time to work out our arrangement and do some digging at the hospital. Someone has information on what happened the night the babies were born, and I'm going to figure out who made this mistake."

"If you need help, I'll be your wingman," Brandon announced. "I'm tougher and smarter than you."

Ryder laughed at his brother's ego shining through even in the middle of an offer of assistance.

His smile faded as his father continued to frown. "I'm sorry, Dad," he said automatically. "I know this is a critical time for the company's future, and I'm letting you down."

"You're not," Chandler answered without hesitation, but Ryder didn't believe him. His dad had expressed disappointment for far less.

"As soon as Esme and I settle into a routine, I'll be back."

"Probably not as CEO," Brandon couldn't help but mutter.

"Stop." Chandler held up a hand to his younger son. "This isn't the time for petty posturing."

"It was a joke," Brandon insisted.

"Not a funny one." Their father turned his attention back to Ryder. "You're doing the right thing. Taking care of your son—both of your boys—takes precedence above everything else."

"It does?" Brandon asked.

At the same time, Ryder agreed, "It does."

"Yes." Chandler gave a decisive nod. "I'm proud of you for having your priorities straight," he continued. "The company will be here when you get back, and nothing will be decided about my position until that time." He glanced at Brandon. "Don't be in too much of a hurry to kick me to the curb, son."

"I'm not," Brandon mumbled, obviously chastised.

"Thank you, Dad." Ryder stood and tried not to gape as the older man came around the side of the desk and offered a fierce—if formal—hug. This wasn't how he'd expected the meeting to go, but he'd take a win wherever he could get it at the moment. He wanted to believe his father's support indicated a positive outcome overall. He needed to believe in something.

"That was fast," Esme said as she opened the door a half hour later. "How was the meeting?"

Bea stood glaring at her from the other side, hands on hips as she tapped an impatient booted toe against the concrete porch. "I sure hope you don't think my interview with a potential chef for the Cowgirl Café went well. All I could think about was whether my sister had been chopped into a million pieces and shoved into her freezer by her baby's biological father."

"Wow," Esme murmured as she stepped back to allow her sister into the house. "Somebody has been listening to too many true crime podcasts."

"Well, what am I supposed to think?" Bea demanded, her voice rising in obvious frustration.

Esme made a hushing sound. "I just got the boys down for a nap. They need some rest."

"The *boys* plural?" Bea spun on her heel. "Are you

telling me you have both babies here? Esme, what in the world happened today?"

"My life changed," Esme answered, then sighed, feeling suddenly exhausted. She'd been running on nothing but emotions and adrenaline since reading the 411 Me report yesterday. Now the reality of what she'd agreed to slammed into her like a bassinet full of concrete blocks.

"So Ryder Hayes just gave you his baby?" Bea looked flabbergasted. "I knew the guy was a player, but I didn't realize he was a heartless cad. What about his wife or girlfriend?"

"He didn't *give* Noah to me," Esme answered in a stage whisper. How could her sister suggest such a thing? "His girlfriend died in a car accident shortly after giving birth."

Bea's big eyes widened even more. "That's awful."

"I know." Esme swallowed, then said, "We're going to raise the boys together."

"Okay, that's preposterous."

"It's *unconventional*, but I love Chase even though we don't share DNA. As soon as I held Noah, I knew he belonged with me. Ryder feels the same way."

"Oh, yeah?" Bea made a point of glancing around the empty living room. "Then where is this paragon of fatherhood?"

"He had some things to take care of at his company."

"Right," her sister said slowly. "How convenient for him to just dump his baby with you. Is he going out for drinks with his womanizing brother? I've seen one of them around town with a different lady on his arm every time."

"Ryder isn't like that."

"How do you know?"

Esme didn't know, but she wanted to trust him. After everything she'd been through, she *needed* to believe she wasn't alone in all of this.

"Come on," Bea coaxed. "Use your head, Es. I know how big your heart is, and you've always put too much stock in fairy tales. I don't want to see you get hurt the way you did with Seth. You need to be real."

Biting down on the inside of her cheek to keep from screaming, Esme gathered the shreds of her tattered composure and nodded. "Trust me. This situation is as real as it gets, and I still have trouble believing it's happening to me. I'm not giving up a chance to raise the two children I love. Raising them with Ryder—who wants to be a good dad—is the best thing I can do."

The doorbell rang, interrupting her tirade, and she stalked toward the door, flinging it open to find Ryder on the other side, holding a large brown take-out bag in his hand. "Sorry it took me so long. I stopped to pick up dinner from Herv's BBQ. I realized I haven't eaten a thing all day, and I'm guessing you might be in the same situation with two babies to look after."

He looked past her to where Bea was staring at the two of them. "Hi." He held up his free hand to wave.

"Come in," Esme told him. "This is my sister, Bea."

"Her *older* sister," Bea clarified. "And very protective."

"It's a pleasure to meet you." He placed the take-out bag on the narrow table next to the door and held out his hand. "Although the circumstances aren't ideal, I guess we'll see quite a lot of each other in the upcoming years."

Bea ignored his outstretched hand as her gaze darted between Ryder and Esme. "You can't be serious. Two strangers don't raise children together."

"Grandma did with Aunt Vanna," Esme pointed out.

"This isn't the same thing," her sister insisted as Ryder shoved his hand into his pocket. He'd changed out of his suit into dark jeans and a gray Henley that hugged his broad shoulders and an incredibly toned chest and arms.

Now was not the time to get distracted by her too hot parenting partner, Esme chastised herself as she focused on her sister. "Dad wouldn't have grown up feeling like he had Peter as a brother if their moms had tried to manage on their own. Ryder and I can be better parents together, Bea. You have to believe me."

When Bea looked like she would continue arguing, Esme held up a hand. "Or don't. That's your choice. But this is mine. Ryder and I are in this together."

She hadn't realized her hands were clenched at her sides until he reached out to hold one of them.

The small gesture of solidarity made her heartbeat accelerate.

"I'm going to take care of your sister," he said, speaking directly to Bea. "And our sons. You have no reason to trust me." He squeezed Esme's fingers. "Neither of you do, but I'm going to work to earn it every day. That much you can take to the bank."

"Speaking of the bank," Bea said to her sister, "or our fairy godbanker, as I like to call her. Have you talked to Freya about this?"

Esme shook her head. She thought about pulling away from Ryder, but her hand felt too right cradled in his grasp. "You're the only one who knows. I need a couple of days to process everything, okay? Then I promise I'll talk to Freya and Asa. Please support me, Bea."

Bea groaned and threw up her hands. "I always support you, little sis." She ran a hand through her long red hair and stepped forward, hugging both Esme and Ryder at the same time. "I'm here for both of you. So when do I get to meet my new nephew?"

"I'll call you tomorrow," Esme promised. "I think the babies need time to adjust to their expanded family, as well."

"Call or text any time." Bea drew back. "You, too, Ryder Hayes. Let me know if you need anything."

Esme nearly smiled at the look of consternation on his face at Bea's words. He didn't seem bothered when her hackles were raised but was clearly disconcerted by her kindness.

"Okay," he agreed slowly.

Bea gave Esme another hug. "Call me," she whispered, then let herself out the front door, leaving Ryder and Esme standing in the living room still holding hands.

The air between them sparked with something she couldn't name, but she yanked her hand back and stepped away. This arrangement would only work if they stayed focused on the boys, which should be simple enough. One baby was a lot of work, so two should keep her busy enough not to fixate on her attraction to Ryder.

Good luck with that, her body and heart whispered at the same time. Esme chose to ignore them both.

Chapter Six

Besides the continued runaround they were receiving from the hospital administrator and attorney after Noah's test confirmed what they already knew, the next three days were the best Ryder could remember in a long time. Sharing parenting responsibilities with Esme, who was calm and competent in the face of blowouts, crying jags and even an unexplained rash on Noah's back, gave him the ability to breathe easy for the first time since he'd held his son in his arms.

He knew he wasn't the most capable parent but hadn't realized how much his obvious lack of skill added to the normal stress of being a new dad. Esme's presence relieved his anxiety as easily as if she were yanking a sheet from the bed.

He couldn't hope to compete with her soothing

presence and natural aptitude for mothering babies, so Ryder became more determined to discover how the mix-up had occurred at the hospital the night his sons were born.

Greg Oachs called or emailed at least once daily, asking the two of them to sign paperwork that would absolve the hospital from responsibility for the mistake. Although neither he nor Esme had any desire to pursue legal action, he wouldn't let the smarmy lawyer off that easily.

In contrast, the hospital administrator, Mary Dill, sounded genuinely apologetic and willing to help, contritely explaining she'd been given strict instructions not to share any information about the on-duty staff back in October.

However, Ryder wasn't giving up, especially since, earlier in the day, Esme had suddenly remembered overhearing that one of the nurses was called Nancy. It hadn't taken long to narrow down the employees with that name working at County Hospital.

Despite knowing it would anger the attorney and administrator, he'd called all three Nancys and discovered that one of them was a labor and delivery nurse who'd remembered the night of the terrible storm and the chaos on the floor after the patients had been moved into their temporary rooms.

He had a meeting scheduled with her tomorrow for breakfast at the diner in town and hoped she could shed some light on the situation or point him in the right direction to get to the bottom of how something with such long-term consequences could have happened.

"Is everything okay?" Esme asked as she came down the steps. "That's a pretty serious frown you're sporting."

Ryder sighed and made a concerted effort to fix his face. "It's been a long day." He hated to admit how familiar a scowl felt for him. But he'd smiled and laughed more since meeting Esme than he had in ages.

He'd always been serious and intense but now wondered whether that was indeed his nature or a result of the constant pressure to succeed he felt from his father, plus the additional challenge of being a single dad.

A few days into his leave of absence, a weight had been stripped from him, replaced by the sweetness of genuinely enjoying the comforting routine of full-time fatherhood. He and Noah came to Esme's each morning and spent the entire day with her and Chase. He loved every minute of it.

But who was he if he wasn't achieving something? Ryder didn't know the answer and was afraid he could never offer the boys what Esme was able to just by being her true self.

"I was just thinking about how to make this situation better. I want answers for us as well as for the boys."

She padded closer and took a seat on the other end of the sofa. Too far, his body silently complained, although Esme had no idea the effect she had on him.

They were always together, making food in the galley kitchen or walking next to each other when they took the boys out in the double stroller he'd purchased at GreatStore. She seemed to think nothing of their arms brushing, or not to notice the way Ryder's libido went on high alert every time he caught her sweet scent in the air.

"I have an idea about how to make our arrangement better—easier for you," she said with a shy smile.

He stared at her and tried to hide his shock. How could she not see how much she tempted him?

"What do you think about the two of you moving in with Chase and me?"

His body went wild, every cell cheering like the Texans had just won the Super Bowl. Was she suggesting what he hoped?

"I don't mean anything romantic, of course," she said on a rush of breath. "We've established the rules for this arrangement, and I plan to honor them. You don't have to worry in that regard."

"You want to follow the rules," he echoed, and his shoulders sagged in disappointment. He masked the reaction with a wide smile. "That's a smart idea." It was the *worst* idea he'd ever heard. "Just so I'm clear, you want us to live together?"

She nodded. "I hope you don't mind me suggesting it. You and Noah are here every day, and even though your apartment isn't far, it would be better—more efficient—if you moved in instead of going back and forth all the time. You can take the guest room, and Noah will stay in the nursery with Chase."

She stifled a yawn. "This will help, especially at night. We can take turns getting up with them overnight. Maybe that way neither of us will be quite so tired."

It made sense from a practical standpoint, and if Ryder were being honest, he liked being at her cozy home more than his sterile apartment.

"I'm sure you have a lease," she continued, "and probably would want to keep your place anyway. You know...in case you're going on a date or whatever."

A blush rose to her cheeks. It wasn't the first or second time Esme had suggested Ryder was missing out on the dating scene in Chatelaine, even though he'd assured her that wasn't the case. He was too consumed with being a dad to think about anything else. Except that wasn't exactly true because lately Esme was also consuming his thoughts.

But if he admitted that, she'd probably rescind her invitation, which could ruin the entire arrangement. She'd been clear about agreeing to parameters regarding who paid for what and how they would make decisions about the boys.

It was smart and practical, and he appreciated her forethought. It was also another reminder of how much better equipped she was for this role than him.

"I like your idea," he said. "Noah and I would love to move in with you and Chase. I promise not to use all the hot water or leave the toilet seat up."

She giggled and then yawned again.

"In fact," he added, "how about if we stay tonight? I can pick up my things tomorrow, but you've been doing the lion's share of caring for the babies—"

"Only because you've been working hard to track down the hospital staff."

He nodded. "I wish I had more to go on. I'm going to ask the nurse, Nancy, about the volunteer no one can remember seeing before or since. Maybe talking about it will jog her memory. She mentioned seeing the older woman with the babies that night."

"One of the two grandma volunteers," Esme murmured, leaning back on the sofa cushion.

Ryder wanted to cradle her head in his arms and tell her she could use him for support, but that might come across a little *too* enthusiastic.

"On the phone, Nancy said that the woman had made an impression on her because she seemed so light on her feet even though she used a cane. But Mary has no record of a second hospital volunteer signing in for a shift that night."

"Do you think this mystery volunteer is involved?" she asked.

He sighed and ran a hand through his hair. "It seems doubtful, but we don't have any better leads."

"Why would someone switch our boys' ID tags on purpose?" Esme asked. The question had plagued Ryder in the same way. "What did you or I ever do to the people in this town?" She suddenly sat up straighter. "But what if it's not about us? We haven't done anything, but could it have something to do with my family? People remember Edgar and Elias—

if not, they've heard the story. According to Freya, many of the miners who were killed still have relatives and descendants in town."

"Why would anyone want to take revenge on you for your grandfather's sins?"

Esme's chin dipped, her long hair falling forward to hide her face from view. "I don't know. But Freya invited us here to make amends for Edgar and Elias's behavior. There could be people who think my siblings, cousins and I don't deserve the help we're getting. We have a direct connection to a tragedy that in so many ways defined this town." Her chest rose and fell with a shaky breath.

"This is not your fault," he said, shifting closer on the sofa and wrapping his arms around her. If there was anything he knew for certain, it was that Esme had nothing to do with the situation they found themselves in now.

She sagged against him like she needed his strength to bolster her own. He would gladly offer that to her. He wanted to provide more, which made no sense. After all, this arrangement wasn't about him. It was for the benefit of the two innocent boys sleeping upstairs.

"Thank you for everything you're doing, Ryder." She pulled away slightly, and her pale green gaze crashed into his. "I'm not sure what I'd do without you."

Her body was soft and warm against him, and once again, the smell of vanilla wafted through his senses, making him feel like they were in a world all by themselves. Awareness clutched at his chest, and her eyes darkened.

He wanted to kiss her so damn badly and would have given in to the desire, except at that moment, Esme's beautiful mouth widened into another yawn, breaking the spell that had him tangled in its grasp. It must have had the same jarring effect on her because she popped up from the couch like she'd just been stung by a bee.

"There's only one bathroom upstairs," she announced, folding her arms over her chest. "I'll leave clean towels on the sink, and there are fresh sheets on the bed in the spare bedroom. If you need anything before tomorrow…"

"I won't," he said definitively because he couldn't very well tell her that the one thing he needed was her in his arms. He motioned to the baby monitor sitting on the coffee table. "I'll take tonight's shift," he offered. "You don't have to worry about a thing."

Esme looked like she wanted to argue but then nodded. "Good night," she whispered and hurried up the stairs.

He stayed on the sofa for a long time after she'd gone to bed, reminding himself over and over that he couldn't give in to the unexpected yet overwhelming attraction he felt for Esme. She was important to him and his son—both of his sons—and he wasn't going to do anything to jeopardize that.

He climbed the stairs slowly, and after checking on the boys, got ready for bed, although sleep didn't come quickly. His thoughts were far too consumed by the beautiful woman sleeping across the hall.

"They're claiming someone switched your baby for another child?" Freya Fortune asked the question with no small sense of incredulity.

"And now, instead of raising one kid," Esme's brother, Asa, added, "you're going to play mom to two of them?"

Esme gripped her coffee cup more tightly and frowned at her older brother. She'd invited Freya and Asa to breakfast at the diner in the heart of downtown so she could explain the situation with Chase and Noah before they heard it from someone else.

It had been a week since her world had been turned upside down, and although she was content to remain in the tiny bubble she and Ryder had created to get to know each other and the boys, who held both of their hearts, it couldn't last. Chatelaine was a tiny town, and word traveled fast in the tight-knit community.

They'd fallen into a routine like it was the most natural thing in the world. He seemed to want a real partnership and pitched in with everything from diaper changing to laundry to housework and meals.

He'd also started ticking off small projects around the house, like her squeaking back door and the bathroom faucet that dripped. But as helpful as the practical side of their arrangement was turning out to be, getting to know Ryder was pure magic.

She'd finally gotten to a point where her breath

didn't catch every time he walked into a room, but the butterflies in her stomach were becoming a real issue. Despite repeatedly reminding herself that they were doing this for the benefit of the boys, she wasn't sure how to stop herself from falling for him.

"I'm not playing at anything," she told Asa. "Ryder and I both love Chase and Noah. I'm honored to be their mother."

Her brother shared a look with Freya, setting Esme's teeth on edge. She understood the situation was unique, but she wanted her family to trust that she was doing the right thing.

"What do you know about Ryder Hayes?" Asa demanded, pointing a slice of bacon in Esme's direction before taking a bite. "Did you do a background check on this stranger before inviting him to live with you?"

"Your brother is right," Freya said gently. "We wouldn't want anyone to take advantage of you or your situation as a single mom."

"Maybe he's after your money," Asa suggested, running a hand through his dark hair. At thirty, he was four years older than Esme and four years younger than Bea. A classic middle child, he was charming and confident in his ability to make friends and go after his dreams.

At the moment, Asa's dream involved buying a dude ranch, although the current owner, the widow Val Hensen, wasn't making it easy for him. Unlike Esme, Asa seemed to have no doubt things would work out the way he wanted in the end.

"I'm not rich," Esme reminded him. "Do you think he's interested in stealing my extra diapers?"

"You *are* a Fortune," Freya insisted. "There are a lot of people who have strong thoughts about our family, especially in this part of Texas."

The older woman's tone held an unexpected edge, and not for the first time, Esme wondered about her great-uncle's widow and what she'd been through. Freya didn't like to talk about herself, instead focusing on how she could help Edgar's and Elias's grandchildren.

She was in her eighties but appeared decades younger with smooth skin, an ash-blond bob and bright green eyes. While she'd been extremely generous with her time and financial support, there was still a bit of distance there, as if Freya wanted to be part of their lives but wasn't exactly sure how to truly open up.

"Ryder is successful in his own right," Esme said, wondering at her fierce sense of protectiveness toward him. "He's vying for the CEO position of his family's company."

Asa snorted. "And probably using you as free childcare for his kid." He paused as he lifted the coffee cup to his lips and added, "For both of his kids, if that's how you want to look at it."

Tears sprang to Esme's eyes, and she bit down on the inside of her cheek to keep them from spilling over. She understood the concerns Asa and Freya were expressing. Those same niggling doubts kept her up at night, adding to her exhaustion as much as caring for two three-month-olds did. Seth had done a number on her ability to trust people and learning more about her paternal grandfather and great-uncle didn't bolster her overall belief in men.

She loved Asa dearly, but he wasn't exactly a poster child for commitment or how to maintain a mature relationship. Her brother was a ladies' man, although he always seemed to remain friends with his exes—everyone loved Asa.

"There's only one way to look at it," she said, gathering her resolve. Doubts could swirl all they wanted when it came to her and Ryder, but she was sure about her commitment to their sons. "Do you consider Chase any less your nephew given what I've just told you?" she asked her brother.

"Hell, no." Asa looked affronted by the suggestion. "I love that kid."

"I know you do." Esme murmured. "So, is there room in your heart for Noah as well?" She picked up her phone from the table. "He looks like you and me when we were babies, Asa."

"I wouldn't care if he had Bea's carrot top or was a dead ringer for the man in the moon." Asa took the phone from her, smiling as he scrolled through her camera roll. "He's family, too. I'm going to teach both those boys to ride a horse and throw a ball and—"

"If Ryder Hayes will allow it," Freya said softly. "Esme isn't in this alone anymore."

"She was *never* alone." Asa shifted the phone so Freya could look at the photos with him.

"I felt alone," Esme admitted. Although her brother looked shocked, it was apparent Freya already had an inkling as to the way Esme had been struggling despite doing her best to appear like she had it all together.

"I understand what Ryder and I are doing seems unorthodox, but it also means that I have someone to share the responsibility of parenthood with. And I needed that more than I let myself acknowledge."

Asa leaned forward, his familiar dark brown eyes shimmering with brotherly affection. "You're my little sister. I'm here for you…whatever you need, Es. I'd like to meet my new nephew and Ryder Hayes, too. This guy needs to know that you are something special and not just because you're available to watch his children."

She shook her head. "That's not how he treats me, Asa. I promise. Ryder has an important job, but he's taking a leave of absence from his company while we transition to this co-parenting thing. Neither of us has all the answers, but he values me. He makes me feel like I'm important to him, and that's a big change from my late husband."

"Rest his soul," Freya murmured.

"Not to speak ill of the dead." Asa rolled his eyes. "But your late husband was an undisputed jerk."

Freya and Esme both chuckled at Asa's plain-spoken assessment.

"You have to say that because you're my brother, but I appreciate it anyway. That's the kind of I've-got-your-back loyalty I want Chase to have with Noah.

We both know that growing up without a father was hard on Dad and Uncle Peter, but they were in it together, and that made a difference." She sighed. "My sons are going to have both a mother and a father. They'll never have any reason to doubt how much we love them. We might not be a typical family, but Ryder and I are dedicated to the boys and making this work."

They all had a few moments to digest the conversation as the waitress came to clear the plates, blatantly flirting with Asa as she did. He had an easy way with women, although he didn't seem interested in being tied down.

Bea's initial comments about Ryder, his brother and dad still lurked in the corners of Esme's mind and heart. It was simple enough to tell herself not to get overly attached to him. Theirs was an arrangement of convenience—just last night over dinner, he'd tentatively suggested they begin the search for a new house, one where they could raise the boys together but each have more privacy. He seemed to think there were options around Chatelaine for properties with multiple dwellings.

The suggestion was a reminder that the situation wasn't merely temporary, but forever. She'd immediately wondered if her worries about him needing space for entertaining potential lady friends might be justified in spite of his denial about wanting to date.

So far, the two of them had been together every night, making dinner in her galley kitchen or ordering carryout. They took the boys on daily walks and had paid a visit to the local bookstore, Remi's Reads, because it turned out that Ryder was as avid of a book nerd as Esme. He was handsome, sweet, successful *and* a reader. Was it any wonder she was drawn to him?

She could also imagine him attracting the attention of eligible women around town the same way her brother did, and she didn't know how she would eventually deal with that and not let him see that it hurt her.

"Do you have an idea of how the switch occurred when no one at the hospital realized it?" Freya asked as she handed her credit card to the waitress. Their great-aunt always insisted on paying, which bothered Esme.

She knew Freya had loads of money, although the older woman chose to live at the Chatelaine Motel, an aged and somewhat shabby motor lodge at the end of town, because she claimed to enjoy the charm of it.

But Esme didn't want her to feel like they only spent time with her because of her financial support and hoped eventually Freya would feel close enough with the Fortunes to open up about her life. Esme's grandma still lived in Cave Creek and remained uninterested in visiting Chatelaine. Ryder was close with his mom, but she lived hours away in Houston. They didn't see each other often based on what he'd shared, particularly given that his father's serial cheating and his parents' eventual divorce had been difficult on his mother. So, as far as

Esme was concerned, Freya was the closest thing her boys would have to a grandma figure living nearby, and she wanted to find a way to forge a meaningful connection in a way that made her great-aunt comfortable.

"Ryder is determined to get to the bottom of who's responsible for what happened that night," Esme said. "Although, I'm not sure it matters. What's done is done, and I don't see the point of dwelling on the past."

Freya's mouth pressed into a thin line. "People need to be held accountable."

"I suppose," she agreed. "But the only lead we have so far is a nurse who remembers an older woman with a volunteer badge hanging around that night."

"Well, no matter what you find out, there's no doubt in my mind that you'll be an excellent mother to Chase and Noah," Asa said, pushing back from the table. He gave Esme a hug that turned into a gentle headlock, one of his signature older brother moves. "I remember when you were a pipsqueak and you played dolls for hours on end."

"You were extremely rude about wrecking my teddy-bear tea parties," Esme retorted as she elbowed him in the ribs.

Freya gave them each an awkward pat on the back. "We should get out of here before the two of you knock into a waitress carrying a tray of dishes."

Esme grinned and blew out a satisfied breath as she led the way out of the diner. This morning was the

Chapter Seven

Ryder wasn't sure how long someone had been knocking at the door before he finally heard it over the persistent wailing of two babies mid-meltdown. He couldn't believe how badly he was struggling to handle Chase and Noah by himself while Esme had breakfast with her brother and great-aunt and then ran errands.

Initially, he'd encouraged her to take the entire day for herself, insisting that he would love the time with their boys. He'd even bristled a bit when she'd seemed unwilling to leave them solely in his care for that long.

The first fifteen minutes of her time away had been without incident. Both babies were down for their morning nap, so Ryder had spent his time re-searching the history of the Fortune family in Chat-

elaine on the internet. He didn't believe the tragedy
of the silver miners could have anything to do with
his baby being switched for Esme's at the hospital,
but her concern was enough to prompt him to learn
more about it.

Through the course of his research, he'd discovered her grandfather's older brother, Wendell, had
returned to town and reconnected with his grandchildren during the past year.

Although he and the fourth Fortune brother of
their generation, Walter, had no involvement with
the accident at Elias and Edgar's silver mine, the
death of those innocent miners had weighed heavily
on Wendell. So much so that he'd assumed a new
identity for many years as a way to distance himself
from the painful past.

Ryder had just started perusing a story on the life
of the mine's foreman, who'd been blamed for the accident by Edgar and Elias, when he heard the sound
of a baby crying through the monitor. By the time he
got to the nursery, both boys were fully awake and
not happy about it, even though Esme had been confident they'd nap for most of the time she was gone.

Ryder had learned quickly that if he could count
on one thing with babies, it was that as soon as he
understood their schedule, the routine would be up-
ended.

He tried not to take it personally that Chase and
Noah cried more with him than they did when Esme
was taking care of them. She repeatedly told him that
crying was a regular part of this stage of their lives,

but he suspected it had something to do with him. They would typically settle after mere moments in Esme's soft, soothing hold, but neither seemed to have any more faith in Ryder than he had in himself.

He opened the door with a screaming baby in each arm and found himself staring at Esme's sister, the one who didn't seem to like him very much.

"Hello!" He shouted to be heard over the crying babies. "Nice to see you again, Bea. Your sister's not at home right now, so you might want to come back when—"

"I know she's not here," Bea interrupted, reaching out to take Noah from him as she stepped into the house. "I'm here to talk to you, Ryder. Apparently, I got here in the nick of time to offer respite childcare. You look like you're about to start sobbing along with these two cuties."

"That's my usual emotional state," he muttered under his breath as he closed the front door, unable to muster embarrassment that a woman he would like to impress, given his relationship with her sister, was seeing him so at a loss.

He might feel confident in his ability to run Hayes Enterprises, although whether he would get a chance to do that remained to be seen, but he had no such certainty in his parenting skills. Esme was the expert, and he'd quickly come to rely on her to take the lead in every aspect of caring for the boys.

Bea couldn't compare with her sister in the baby whisperer department, but between the two of them, the boys eventually quieted. Ryder placed Chase in the motorized swing that sat in the middle of the kitchen, and the baby yawned and then stuck his fist in his mouth.

"I can take Noah if you'd like," Ryder offered, but Bea shook her head.

"Have you seen pictures of Esme or our brother, Asa, when they were this age?"

"I haven't yet."

"He looks just like the two of them. The resemblance is striking." She stared at Noah in amazement.

"He's lucky to look like his mother. She told me everything left from your parents' house has been put into a storage unit. Once we're more settled, I'll take her to Cave Creek to move what she wants to Chatelaine. I think it's important to Esme to have some of those family things here."

"You're right," Bea said slowly, then glanced over at Chase, who was losing the fight to keep his eyes open. "Now I know where he got the cleft in his chin. I had assumed it was from his father's side of the family."

"It was," Ryder confirmed, wanting to clarify that no other man would play that role in either of the children's lives.

"My sister has a big heart." Bea gazed at Noah as she spoke, although the words were clearly meant for Ryder. "Her husband took advantage of that. He took advantage of her under the mistaken assumption that she had access to...well, a fortune, given our last name."

"I'm not interested in Esme's money," Ryder answered, affronted at the suggestion. "I have plenty of my own."

"So, in what way are you interested in her exactly?" Bea demanded, dropping a kiss on Noah's forehead.

He resisted the urge to fidget. There was no way anyone could have guessed that he was often nearly done in by his attraction to Esme. "Has she explained our arrangement to you?"

"Right down to the rules. I was surprised the two of you have already agreed you're free to date other people."

"Did we agree to date other people?" he murmured. "I don't remember that."

Bea looked amused. "Esme read your rules to me."

"*Her* rules," Ryder clarified. "You saw the state I was in here. Do I look like somebody who would be a big draw as a date?"

"Either that's a rhetorical question, or you don't own a mirror."

Ryder felt color race to his cheeks. "I wasn't fishing for a compliment, and I'm not interested in dating." At least, not other women if Esme was a possibility.

"And what exactly is your interest in my baby sister?" Bea Fortune asked the question lightly, but Ryder got the impression she expected a serious answer. Was he so transparent in his interest?

"Obviously, I don't know Esme well yet, but I like her, and more importantly, I respect her. She's a great mother and has handled this situation with a huge amount of care and maturity. She's someone

I'd like to emulate as far as how a parent should act in the face of a crisis."

He cleared his throat. "I'm never going to do anything to hurt her if that's what you're worried about."

"You're right. She's an amazing mother and has a heart the size of this great state we live in. She considers both of these boys her sons, and it doesn't matter which one she brought home after giving birth or which one shares her DNA. Noah and Chase are hers as far as Esme is concerned."

"I feel the same way." Ryder inclined his head and studied Bea. "Is there something I've done or Esme has told you I've done that gives you a different impression? I feel like we're dancing around a topic, and I'm a couple of steps behind."

The pretty redhead shifted but didn't drop her gaze from Ryder's. He respected her for that. "You're relatively new to Chatelaine. So are we. I'm not sure if Esme mentioned that I'm opening a restaurant in town?"

"She did. She's very proud of you and your brother."

Bea smiled. "The feeling is mutual. I've met a lot more people than she has at this point. The men in your family have a reputation around town already. I'm not sure if it's gossip or has been earned, but it doesn't mesh with the kind of person I want my sister to have in her life."

Ryder's stomach churned. He knew what that reputation would be, and although he'd guessed and expected this news, he still hated to think that Esme might believe him to be a player. No wonder she went out of her way to clarify that she was willing to give him space to date.

"She doesn't know I'm here if you were wondering," Bea offered. "I just wanted to—"

"Vet me?"

"Speak to you," she countered.

He nodded, and although he didn't appreciate people making assumptions about him, he understood the concern. He also liked that Esme had people looking out for her because, with her gentle soul, he imagined she had the self-preservation instincts of a kitten.

"Your sister can make her own decisions, but I meant it when I said I respect her and I'm not going to hurt her." He should leave it at that. Because while he understood Bea's protectiveness, he didn't owe her anything. Still, he added, "I'm not like my father or brother. Not in the ways that would impact my ability to live up to my end of the bargain or be the kind of father these two deserve."

Bea was silent for a moment, then smiled and visibly relaxed. "I like you, Ryder Hayes, and I didn't expect to. Thank you for being so honest, and if it's not too much trouble—"

"I won't mention this visit to Esme," he promised.

She snuggled Noah for another minute, then transferred him to his father's arms. Ryder half expected the boy to wake immediately and cry again, but Noah remained blissfully asleep. Chase had also fallen asleep in the swing. He should move both boys

upstairs to their shared crib, but he was too worried
about waking them again.

After locking the door behind Esme's sister, he
returned to the couch and made himself comfortable
while he watched his two sons.

For the first time in his life, striving for success
or his father's love wasn't first on his list of priorities. Instead, he enjoyed this moment and the opportunity to appreciate how special it was to have not
one but two sons in addition to the woman at his side
helping to raise them. The time had come to finally
allow himself to become the man he wanted to be.

Esme blinked awake in the darkness, heart pounding like she'd just run a fifty-yard dash. She was confused and disoriented for a few terrifying moments,
the nightmare holding her in its grip.

In her dream, she'd returned to the night she gave
birth, and the storm had raged even more violently.
There'd been two bassinets at the end of her bed, but
instead of a nurse checking on her babies, the older
volunteer Ryder was intent on tracking down had
slowly entered the room, cane in hand and her vivid
blue eyes glittering with an emotion Esme couldn't
name.

The woman had shaken her head at Esme as if
admonishing her. Then she hooked the crook of
her cane over the edge of one of the bassinets and
wheeled it out of the room. The relentless crack of
thunder drowned Esme's scream as she watched one
of her precious children being taken from her.

Her body quivering with residual fear, she climbed out of bed and silently made her way across the dark hall. Although she knew the dream wasn't real, she had to check on Chase and Noah and see for herself that both boys were safe.

The nursery door was slightly ajar, causing panic to flare inside her, but the band around her chest loosened as she pushed it open to reveal Ryder standing in the middle of the room, a swaddled baby tucked under each arm.

He swayed back and forth, singing what sounded to Esme like a quiet rendition of "Born in the USA." He wore a white T-shirt and gray athletic shorts, his hair tousled from sleep. Maybe it was her own exhaustion or the leftover adrenaline her dream had produced, but she'd never seen a sexier sight.

She must have made a sound, or he sensed her presence because his gaze collided with hers, green eyes sparking with awareness.

"What are you doing up?" he asked, his voice soft. "I'm on duty tonight."

"Bad dream," she answered and stepped into the room. "The mystery volunteer from the hospital was trying to take one of the boys."

The description didn't convey the panic the nightmare manufactured inside her, but Ryder must have understood how bad it had been. He moved toward her and wordlessly transferred Noah to her arms.

Esme sighed as she drew the baby closer and leaned down to breathe in his sweet scent.

"No one's going to take either of them." Ryder was

so close she could feel the warmth of his body and took comfort in his vow. It was easy to believe everything would be fine with this man to protect her.

Undoubtedly, he'd use his strength and power to keep Noah and Chase safe, but who was going to protect Esme's heart when she was so vulnerable to losing it?

They stood together for a minute, their arms brushing as they rocked back and forth. Then she began to sing a lullaby her mother had favored when Esme was a girl. "'Hush, little baby, don't say a word,'" she crooned. The classic song might not have the same resonance as a selection from the Springsteen catalog, but each of the boys smiled in their sleep as she continued with the verses, whether in response to her voice or their private dreams, she couldn't say.

When the last note ended, they placed the babies in their shared crib. Ryder had moved Noah's crib from his apartment to the nursery, but the boys slept better when they were close together, so until that changed, Chase and Noah slept side by side in their swaddles.

Ryder placed a hand on Esme's back as they left the room, and his touch pulsated through her, making her knees weak. As the door clicked shut, she turned, ready to apologize for her silly overreaction to a dream.

However, the heat in his eyes had the words catching in her throat.

"You're so damn beautiful," he said, shaking his

head like the words pained him to say. "I don't know what to do next, Esme."

She had a few ideas, but it wasn't easy to fathom he felt the same about her.

Then he reached up and threaded his fingers through her long hair. His chest rose and fell in shallow breaths as if touching her undid something in him. It certainly had that effect on Esme.

Longing coursed through her like a rushing stream, and she wasn't sure how to dam up her desire. Her mouth had gone dry, and she licked her lips, causing Ryder to let out a soft groan in response.

She lifted onto her toes and kissed him, unable to resist and unwilling to worry about the consequences. This moment felt precious, and she had to believe the quiet night and the bond they already shared would keep her safe.

Either that or she'd deal with the eventual consequences, but not now. All she wanted was to savor the taste of him and how perfectly they fit together. He cupped her face and angled her head to deepen the kiss as Esme spread her palms over the hard planes of his chest.

She could feel his heart beating a frantic rhythm under the thin fabric of his shirt, but it wasn't enough. Her body seemed to have a mind of its own, and her yearning surged to become a full-blown torrent of need.

Their tongues melded, and she lost herself in the moment even as her hands slipped under his shirt to move up and over his back. He trailed kisses along her jaw and neck, one finger tracing the sensitive dip of her collarbone.

Her pajama top was blessedly a scoop neck, and it felt like heaven when Ryder tugged on it and gently kissed the top of her breast.

Esme was ready to shuck the cotton fabric over her head, but the sound of a baby's sudden cry split the air. Both she and Ryder jumped back like two teenagers discovered in the basement by angry parents.

They stood silently for several seconds, but whichever boy cried out had also settled himself. It didn't matter. The interruption reminded Esme that there were more important things to consider than her red-hot desire for Ryder Hayes.

"That can't happen again," she said, unsure whether she was hoping to convince him or herself.

She could see Ryder's thick brows draw together in the pale light from the moon shining in the window at the end of the short hallway. He looked like he wanted to argue, but after a few more charged moments of tense silence, he nodded.

"Whatever you want," he answered, which was not the response she'd expected.

Esme figured he'd understand that nothing could happen between them but quickly realized that physical intimacy probably didn't mean the same thing to Ryder as it did to her.

He meant something to her that went beyond kissing or even sex. The way he listened to her, laughed at her silly jokes and truly seemed to respect her as a person was more of a gift than Esme could have expected to receive.

Ryder had made it clear they were together because it was the right thing for raising the boys. But she was a woman built for love and commitment and could not risk letting him capture any more of her heart. Not with the future they'd committed to sharing.

"Good night," she said and retreated to her bedroom, pressing her back to the door as she listened to the door across the hall close a few seconds later.

At least Esme wouldn't have to worry about any more nightmares tonight. Sleep would be a long time coming with the memory of Ryder's mouth on hers branded into her heart and mind.

Chapter Eight

"Are you sure about this?" Esme asked the following Monday afternoon as she stared up at the rustic yet elegant exterior of the LC Club.

The weekend's unseasonably warm temperatures and sunny days had morphed into an overcast start to the week, one Ryder refused to take as an omen.

"I'd like you to meet my father and brother," he told her. "Although today you're just going to be getting Brandon because Dad missed his flight home from Miami last night."

Whether Chandler had accidentally gotten the time wrong or chosen to take an extra day in the warm and sunny weather of South Florida, Ryder didn't care to hazard a guess. It wouldn't have been the first time his dad had extended a work trip to include a three-day weekend, especially when in a location filled with an ever-present bevy of beautiful women.

It shouldn't come as a surprise. His father claimed that welcoming Chase and Esme to the Hayes family in whatever way their arrangement allowed was a priority, but Ryder knew the man too well to believe that.

"I appreciate that," Esme said as she took Noah's infant carrier from Ryder, leaving him with Chase's. "I want to meet them as well, but we could have planned a dinner at the house like we did with Bea and Asa."

Ryder swallowed against the uncomfortable emotions that burned his throat. "The difference is you enjoy your siblings. I did, too. Asa and Bea are great. I'm just sorry your great-aunt had to cancel."

"Me, too," Esme agreed. "Freya texted this morning and said her headache is much better, and she wants to meet you and Noah soon."

Maybe that was true, or maybe Freya Fortune was working from the same playbook as Chandler Hayes.

"Very soon. But it's better to spend time with my brother somewhere public." He hadn't shared with Brandon or his dad that he and Noah had moved into Esme's house or anything about his hunt for a property they could buy together that would give them each more privacy.

He also had yet to convince Esme that a move would benefit her as much as him. If the kiss they'd shared the other night hadn't proved that he had no interest in dating anyone else, he wasn't sure what would.

Esme nodded but still appeared hesitant. "This place seems even fancier up close than it does from where I can see it on my walks around the lake."

"My dad decided to make it the jewel in the Hayes Enterprises' crown because of the location and the potential he sees in Chatelaine. I'd like to focus on improving the club's already impeccable customer service and the attention to detail the staff offers. That's what makes a property special, and if we have everyone in the company from the top down committed to that vision, it will benefit all of us as well as the bottom line."

Ryder had walked several paces before he realized Esme was no longer in step beside him. He glanced over his shoulder to find her staring at him, a smile playing around the edges of her lips.

"What's wrong?"

"You need to go back to work."

"I told you I'm going to take some extra time off. I don't want you to feel like I'm leaving you in the lurch. These boys are both of our responsibilities, and I'm going to prove to you that I take it seriously."

Ryder also needed to prove that he wasn't as incompetent a parent as he felt each time he compared himself to Esme. Just last night, he'd accidentally pinched Noah's chubby thigh while buttoning the boy's pajamas.

Esme had assured him that the angry half circle of tender pink flesh was something either of them could have caused. Even so, Ryder had been gutted by his son's cries, especially when the baby seemed to struggle to gulp in air, which Esme also claimed was a normal thing babies did when they were crying too hard. He'd never heard Noah, who was typically calm and content, cry like that.

She was kind enough to refrain from mentioning that Noah was wailing so hard because of Ryder's ineptitude. Sometimes, he wasn't sure why Esme would bother to keep him around. How had he managed to handle fatherhood before her?

Between his family's reputation and his deficiencies, plus the fact that he'd clearly shocked her with the level of his desire in the hallway, she had to know she could manage parenthood on her own just as easily as having to coach him through it. He wondered if encouraging him to return to work was a shrewd attempt to get him out of her hair.

"Your dad hasn't decided on the CEO position," she reminded him. "I can't comment on your brother yet, but I know you'd be a fantastic choice to run the company. Don't give up your dreams or aspirations, Ryder. They're important."

"Not as important as being a father," he countered, willing her to believe him.

"Just consider it," she pleaded and reached out to squeeze his arm. "It's okay to want both."

He nodded tightly but didn't answer. Was it okay to want her most of all?

They entered the club and took the stairs to the second-floor restaurant overlooking the banks of

Lake Chatelaine that served lunch on weekdays. He introduced her to a few of his coworkers, proud to have Esme at his side. She wore a navy-colored dress with pleats around the skirt. It flowed over her luscious curves and stopped just below her knees, and she'd paired it with tan ballet flats and pulled her hair into a low ponytail.

Despite the demure look, he found himself riveted by her shapely ankles and the delicate heart pendant she wore around her neck.

He might have it bad when it came to Esme, but at least she wasn't the type of woman his brother would typically notice. Ryder held out hope that Brandon would behave himself and treat her with the level of respect she deserved.

As it turned out, Ryder had been worried about the wrong thing. Brandon was not only kind to Esme, but the jerk also blatantly flirted with her. Granted, Ryder had no claim to her other than in his secret fantasies, but she was clearly important to him.

Brandon knew that, so his flirtation made him feel like diving over the glasses of sparkling water and sweet iced tea and tackling his brother to the polished wood floor of the club's dining room.

He should have expected this. Brandon was like an annoying truffle pig who could snuffle out anything meaningful to Ryder so he could take it for himself.

Esme appeared flustered and amused by the younger Hayes brother's charm. She laughed at his jokes and beamed when Brandon played peek-a-boo with the two babies, whose carriers had been fastened in infant seat cradles next to each other at the table.

"How are you adjusting to life in Chatelaine?" Esme asked Brandon after the food was brought to the table—cheeseburgers for Ryder and Brandon and a club sandwich for her. "The pace of life here must feel slow compared to what you're used to in Houston."

"I like that there's no traffic," Brandon said, popping a fry into his mouth. "The local highways feel like they're made for hitting the gas pedal. Have you ever driven a Porsche, Esme?"

She giggled. "I can't say I've ever had the opportunity."

"We're going to have to remedy that," Ryder's irritating brother said with a wink. "Daddy Daycare over there—" he pointed toward Ryder but didn't take his eyes off Esme. "—can babysit while we go for a drive."

"It's not babysitting," Ryder said through clenched teeth, "when I'm their father."

"Sure, sure," Brandon agreed. "Everyone in town is so nice, and it's obvious you're no different, Esme. Do you like picnics? I could take you on a picnic."

Ryder sniffed. "I can take her on a picnic."

"I asked first," Brandon countered.

"So what?"

Esme held up her hands, palms out. "Hold on. There's no need to argue about a hypothetical picnic." She grimaced. "Is this what we have to look forward to with Chase and Noah?"

"No," Ryder answered at once. "Our boys are going to be friends."

"What the...?" Brandon looked legitimately hurt, which made Ryder's gut clench. "We're friends, bro."

Ryder shook his head to clear it, unable to believe what he was hearing. He loved Brandon but had never considered them friends. "Then why do you always try to best me in every way?"

Ryder placed his napkin over his plate, stomach suddenly churning too much to think about eating. "I understand Dad set us up for that when we were kids, but we're grown men, Bran."

"You're my big brother. I don't want to best you." Brandon laughed and loosened his tie like it was choking him. "I want to *be* you. I always have. Clearly, Dad wanted that, too, so he pushed me to do everything you did. I could never be you, so I had to be better."

If Brandon had revealed he was heading off to join a monastery, Ryder couldn't have been more shocked.

Had he made a terrible mistake in keeping his distance? Had he let their father's behavior influence his feelings to the point that he'd missed out on being closer with his brother? Could he make it better now? What would he risk if he tried?

"I love knowing this about the both of you," Esme told them with a wide smile. "I could tell you shared a bond, even if it was messed up for a while. It's how I want Chase and Noah to grow up, only..." she grabbed Ryder's hand "...how about we skip all that business about competition and pitting them against one another?"

He nodded numbly while Brandon roared with laughter.

"Oh, you're a keeper," his brother told Esme. "You're going to be good for too-serious-never-cracks-a-smile Ryder. I can tell."

"I smile," Ryder proclaimed with a frown.

"Maybe when you pass gas like a baby. Otherwise, it's all business." Brandon leaned toward Esme like he was revealing a secret. "The crazy part is people love him for it. Almost every day, I bring in a treat for the staff. This week was doughnuts on Monday and cookies on Wednesday. I even rented a karaoke machine for an office happy hour last Friday night."

Esme focused on Brandon but didn't let go of Ryder's hand. He was grateful for her steadying touch.

"That must have been so much fun," she said.

"Not one of them can carry a tune, although that didn't stop the sales staff from belting out the worst songs imaginable. But as much effort as I put into being the fun boss, apparently, I need to bulk order rubber bracelets that say WWRD. That's the theme of the office—'What would Ryder do?'"

"I told him he should return to work," Esme confided, her head close to Brandon's so that it also appeared as if she were sharing something private.

Ryder tapped his own chest like he needed to make sure he wasn't invisible. "You both know I'm sitting right here."

"Yeah. You're hard to miss." Brandon waved a hand in Ryder's direction. "But I'd much rather focus on your better half."

He liked the sound of Esme being his better half, as if they shared a true partnership. To Brandon's credit, he cut back on the flirting, and the remainder of the lunch was actually enjoyable.

How could she make everything better—even the relationship with his brother that had been antagonistic as long as he could remember?

He hadn't given much thought to how he'd contributed to the animosity between them, but as he watched Esme laugh at Brandon's wild stories and running litany of jokes, Ryder saw his sibling in a new light.

Maybe there was more to Brandon than the shallow, slick, skirt-chasing role he seemed to embody like a second skin. He was fun and funny, and he had a way of making people feel comfortable that didn't come naturally to Ryder.

Although they were barely old enough to have personalities, he could already see differences between Chase and Noah. Noah might share DNA with Esme, but he was an observer like Ryder, often studying the world around him with his brows furrowed like he needed to make sense of every aspect.

On the other hand, Chase liked to pump his arms and legs as if he couldn't wait to start moving and shaking.

Ryder would do his best to encourage both boys to be their best selves and each other's staunchest ally.

Maybe he would have learned to laugh more if his dad had given him and Brandon that gift.

"It was great to meet you," Brandon told Esme as they rose from the table after the dishes had been cleared and the check paid. He thwacked Ryder on the shoulder. "Always a pleasure, bro. Take all the time you need away from the office." He winked. "That'll give me the time I need to ensure I'm chosen as Dad's successor. Don't worry though... I'm going to be a great boss. You'll love working for me."

Brandon grinned as he made the pledge, but Ryder didn't see the humor in it. He was about to offer a stinging retort when he felt Esme place a gentle hand on his back.

"I imagine the two of you will do great things working *together*," she said with a pointed look at his brother.

"Right," Brandon agreed, winking again. Did he have something in his damn eye? "That's what I meant to say. I'll talk to you soon, Ry. Esme, that offer for a ride is always open."

Ryder narrowed his eyes and resisted the urge to growl low in his throat as his brother sauntered away. He followed Esme out of the restaurant and down the stairs, unsure whether he wanted to throttle Brandon or try to repair their relationship. Both felt like viable options.

"Here's the plaque you mentioned." Esme stopped in front of the small memorial to the fifty miners who'd died in the tragic accident years earlier. "It bothers me that my grandfather's greed caused something like this. Growing up, we didn't hear much about him or Uncle Elias. I never gave either of them much thought. When Freya talks about my great-uncle, it's obvious how much she loved him. I don't know that anything my generation can do to contribute to the Chatelaine community will right the wrongs of the past."

He took her hand. "That isn't your responsibility, and I believe everything you do makes the world a better place."

The golden flecks in her green eyes shimmered as she smiled at him. "You're too nice, Ryder."

He barked out a laugh. "No one has ever accused me of that before."

They continued toward the parking lot, and Chase began to fuss as they latched the car seats to their bases in the back seat, while Noah had fallen asleep in his.

Esme smoothed a hand over Chase's cheek and then offered him a pacifier, which quieted him. "I think Chase is going to be our social butterfly." She settled herself in the passenger seat and fastened her seat belt. "It's funny how those two can be so much alike yet have their own distinct personalities. It was nice to meet your brother today."

"Do you want to go out with him?" The question popped out before Ryder could stop it.

Esme laughed like he was making a joke. "Oh, sure. That's a good one."

"I'm serious," he said, focusing on the road before him as he pulled out of the LC Club parking lot. "I guess I am too serious. You laughed a lot with Brandon. I liked hearing it."

"Your brother is entertaining."

"He's fun," Ryder admitted gruffly. "I should be more fun." He glanced over when she didn't immediately answer. "It's fine if you want to take a ride with him. Driving his Porsche roadster is the definition of fun."

"Not my definition," she said softly. "I don't want to go out with your brother."

Her tone sounded like he'd hurt her feelings, which was the last thing he wanted.

He gripped the steering wheel more tightly. "I just meant—"

"Do you know what fun is to me?" she asked, adjusting the seat belt so she could turn toward him. "Having an extra ten minutes to finish a chapter in the amazing book I'm reading because you offered to put the boys down for their nap. Or when one of them hits a milestone, and we're both there to see it."

"How about when Noah realized he could get his toe into his mouth for the first time like it was the greatest discovery in the history of man or baby?"

Her grin warmed his heart.

"Yes, *that*'s what I find fun, Ryder. I liked getting to know your brother, and I'm excited, although a bit nervous, to meet your dad. But please don't make me part of whatever ongoing competition the two of you have. From this outsider's perspective, it's clear that you each have something different to bring to the CEO position. I'm sure it's going to be a difficult decision for your father, but no matter who he chooses, you and Brandon will still need to work together."

"You heard what he said about being my boss," Ryder insisted, hating that he sounded like a petulant schoolboy or maybe a big brother short on patience. Old habits were hard to break.

"I'm not sure he knows how to relate to you differently." She tapped a finger on her chin. "Is it possible you're dealing with a similar issue?"

Yes, and Esme Fortune was smart to realize it. It was also distinctly probable he was falling for her. Ryder knew he could figure out how to deal with his brother. However, his feelings for Esme were a different story.

Chapter Nine

"Are you sure you don't want to hold one of them?" Esme asked Freya, who looked as shocked as if she'd been asked to hold a venomous snake.

Esme had finally convinced Ryder to end the workweek with a day at the office and made plans to meet Freya and Wendell Fortune at the small café situated inside GreatStore after she and great-uncle's widow finished their latest shopping trip.

Freya might not feel comfortable with either of Esme's babies, but she certainly liked spending money on them. She'd bought several new toys and some clothes for Noah and Chase, reasoning that it would be cute to dress them in matching outfits for Valentine's Day, which was fast approaching.

The whole town was decked out in pink and red decorations. Many of the displays in GreatStore featured Valentine-themed merchandise, and a pop-up flower shop took center stage near the big-box store's front entrance.

Pushing the double stroller through the automatic doors, Esme remembered that it was around this time last year that she'd found out she was pregnant. When she'd first shared the news with Seth, he'd seemed overwhelmed but excited and committed to her and their unborn child. She refused to compare his behavior with Ryder's, reminding herself that Ryder hadn't done anything to warrant her mistrust. But she'd been betrayed, and it was difficult not to worry that she might be taken advantage of again if she let down her guard.

It had been Seth's idea to get married quickly. The Dallas courthouse where they'd exchanged vows had been filled with leftover Valentine's decorations, even though the holiday had fallen a couple of weeks before their official ceremony.

Was it any wonder the displays of love and romance made her feel a little queasy? She hadn't even been able to muster any eagerness for the new shipment of romance novels that had arrived on her doorstep a few days prior, instead borrowing one of Ryder's thrillers for their evenings on the couch.

She'd been satisfied living in the make-believe world of books for so long. But being deserted by her husband, then finding out he hadn't been faithful for even a brief time, had soured her on the belief in happily-ever-afters.

She had been dealing just fine with the lack of

romance in her life until Ryder Hayes came along, embodying everything she wanted in a hero.

The kiss they'd shared had rocked her to her core, but it had been a mistake. Her body didn't agree, but her heart was already so lost to Ryder—how could she take the risk of complicating their partnership even more?

Besides, he didn't seem the least bit interested in repeating the kiss. Although she couldn't seem to help finding excuses to take his hand or brush up against him, she noticed that he pulled away as soon as possible.

Forcing her attention back to the present, she smiled as Wendell Fortune cooed at Noah, who sat contentedly in the older man's arms.

"I'm gonna leave the baby holding to this guy." Freya murmured, hitching a polished nail in Wendell's direction. "I'm not a baby person."

"Turns out I've got a way with the little ones." Wendell scrunched up his face and then stuck out his tongue at Noah, whose blue eyes widened as he flashed a gummy grin. "I'm glad to have a chance to know the offspring of my brothers. It gives an old man a heap of pleasure to know that, despite everything, you and your siblings and cousins turned out good. Your grandfather and great-uncle would have been proud."

It was silly to be grateful for the approval of a relative she'd only recently met, but Wendell's words delighted Esme. She wasn't sure of his actual age, but he seemed quite a bit older than Freya, and Esme knew he was dealing with some heart health issues. In contrast, her great-aunt was trim and spry, her hair curled in a becoming shorter style that framed her face.

She wore jeans and a soft sweater that looked more on trend with current fashion than most of the clothes Esme owned. On the other hand, Wendell appeared weathered and walked slowly, his shoulders slightly stooped.

Esme knew he was worth millions even after bequeathing much of his fortune to his grandchildren, but he didn't look wealthy or act snobbish like some of the people she'd seen during her lunch with Ryder and Brandon at the LC Club.

"Wendell is right," Freya confirmed. "Your generation of the Fortunes is more deserving of the family's legacy in this state and this town than your great-uncle or grandfather were." She fiddled with one of her delicate hoop earrings and spoke in a hushed tone as she added, "You're good kids."

Her voice broke on the last word, like the fact that she might be coming to care for her late husband's family truly surprised her. "I wish things would have turned out differently, especially for those fifty families who lost loved ones in the mining tragedy."

"Or perhaps fifty-one families," Esme said as Chase finished off the bottle she was feeding him. She lifted the boy onto her shoulder and patted his back. "Asa told me that last summer, they found a note near the castle where the number fifty is etched into the concrete to honor the miners."

"There were fifty-one," Freya said tightly, repeating the phrasing of the note. "I heard about that, but it's ridiculous."

"I'm not sure the rumors have merit," Wendell acknowledged. "But I'm checking it out. In fact, Devin Street called me the other day to ask for an on-record comment about this new development to an old story."

"The owner of the *Chatelaine Daily News* is interested in the note?" Esme let out a low whistle. "Does that mean there's an official investigation?"

"I hope not," Freya snapped, then offered an apologetic smile when Esme and Wendell looked at her in surprise. "It feels like a waste of time. Why would an additional death be brought up after all this time?"

Wendell pointed a finger at her like she'd hit the nail on the head. "Devin told me it got his attention. I think he believes where there's smoke, there must be fire."

"But who would the mystery missing person be?" Freya asked. "It doesn't make sense. Everyone in the mine shaft was accounted for that day. I knew those men and—" She cleared her throat. "Not personally, of course, and Elias didn't like to speak of the tragedy. But I read up on it, so I felt like I knew the men."

"Walter and I did, too," Wendell agreed. "Although we were busy with our business ventures at the time, I wish I'd paid more attention to what my brothers were doing. I knew they'd overheard our conversation about finding gold around Chatelaine but never dreamed they'd take the risks they did to make more money."

"I wish you'd known him the way I do," Freya said softly, then amended, "The way I did."

"I get it." Esme reached across the table, but at the last moment, Freya pulled her hand into her lap. She was generous but a hard nut to crack sometimes.

"Sometimes, it feels like my parents are still with us," Esme said, drumming her fingers on the cool Formica, "even though they've been gone over five years now. Things weren't the happiest growing up, but I loved them."

"The ones we love stay close in our hearts," Wendell agreed, then touched a fingertip to Noah's nose. "Along with the new loves we discover."

Esme knew Wendell was talking about babies, but an image of Ryder filled her mind. Her phone pinged with an incoming text, and she welcomed the distraction.

"Speaking of new love, Bea apologizes for being unable to join us this morning. She's finishing up a meeting about the new restaurant." Esme grinned at Freya. "I think you've introduced my sister to her one true love, the Cowgirl Café. I don't know if she's told you, but our mom once dreamed of opening a restaurant. You're helping Bea honor our family in multiple ways, Freya."

"I'm happy to do it," the older woman answered, although she looked anything but happy at the moment. Esme figured that could be blamed on the way her heart still grieved for Elias, and decided to change the subject.

"My sister's food is sure to be a hit around here. She has such a clear vision for the restaurant."

Wendell chuckled. "And she promised to put meat-loaf on the menu in my honor. It's my favorite."

"It's Elias's favorite, too," Freya shared. "It *was* his favorite," she corrected.

Esme's heart ached for the older woman. Despite her great-uncle's unsavory past, it was apparent Freya had loved him dearly. Sometimes it felt as if the older woman couldn't truly accept that her husband was gone.

"Like you said, I wish we'd gotten to know him." Esme returned a drowsy Chase to his infant carrier. "But at least we have you. You're a blessing in our lives, Freya."

Her great-aunt looked uncomfortable at the compliment. "I haven't done much."

"But you've done *something*," Wendell said as he handed Noah to Esme. "Which is more than my brothers ever did."

Esme glanced at Freya, whose face had gone white as a sheet.

"What's wrong?"

"Nothing," she insisted, but Esme didn't believe her.

"You really have helped us so much. Without you, I never would have thought to get Chase's DNA tested. You helped me discover what I might not have otherwise known. In the process, I found a father for both of them."

Freya's smile was grim. "I don't think you should give me credit."

"Any news on figuring out what happened that night?" Wendell interjected, scrubbing a craggy hand over his jaw.

Esme adjusted Noah's bib and shook her head. "Unfortunately, no. One of the nurses Ryder talked to said two volunteers were working on the labor and delivery floor when the boys were born. We're meeting with the second woman early next week. She's in Florida right now visiting her daughter."

Wendell nodded. "That seems promising."

"Of course, we also received a terse email from the hospital's attorney telling us to cease and desist from contacting their staff members because it's a form of harassment."

"You wouldn't have to take matters into your own hands," Wendell scoffed, "if they were doing anything to handle it."

Freya stood and helped Wendell up from his chair. "Perhaps you should let it go," she suggested with a shrug. "Does it really matter what happened in the grand scheme of things?"

"Hell, yes, it matters." Wendell got to his feet, his movements stiff. "If I know one thing for certain, it's that secrets and lies don't do a damn bit of good. This family has had too many of those, and they've come close to tearing us apart."

Esme nodded, although in some ways, she agreed with Freya. Ryder seemed almost consumed with finding out the details of the switch and who was responsible. She couldn't help but wonder if his anger and irritation over the situation they'd been thrust into drove his determination.

She was trying her hardest not to get caught up in fairy-tale fantasies when it came to their practical and far-too-platonic partnership. Yet he couldn't seem to release the need to find someone to blame. What would happen if he never got to the bottom of it? Would his frustration transfer to Esme?

She hoped that wouldn't be the case. Wendell hugged her, and Freya offered an awkward pat on the arm as they said goodbye.

Esme stopped to catch up with her friend Lily Perry, who worked at the café in GreatStore and had helped Esme choose some items for Chase's nursery.

Lily cooed over both babies and commented on how refreshed Esme looked as the mother of two infants. It was easy to give credit to Ryder. He was a good dad, though he didn't seem to believe that about himself.

Halfway through Esme's recitation of Ryder's best qualities, Lily grabbed her hand. "You like this guy!" the slender brunette with the adorable freckles dotted across her nose exclaimed.

"I hope so." Esme gave what she prayed was a lighthearted laugh. "We're raising two kids together."

"That's not what I mean. You *really* like him, the way a woman likes a man."

"That would be foolish of me," Esme said, which wasn't exactly a denial. "Ryder doesn't see me that way. Besides, the boys are my priority, and I won't do anything to jeopardize the arrangement we've made."

"Foolish or not…"

"Don't say anything," Esme begged. "Not to anyone. It's so silly. I blame hormones."

Lily squeezed her fingers. "Hormones can be blamed for a lot of things, but it's not silly. The two of you are spending almost all your time together. He sounds great, and you're amazing. Why wouldn't it work?"

"I'm not his type," Esme whispered, hating how the words felt like sandpaper on her tongue. "I doubt you could understand falling for someone who doesn't see you like that but—"

"Don't be too sure," Lily interrupted and gave Esme a quick hug. "But the man you describe doesn't sound like a fool, and he'd be one if he weren't already half in love with you."

Esme rolled her eyes. "I wish, or maybe I don't. I've tried love before, and I prefer the kind I read about in romance novels. Less heartache that way."

Lily grinned. "Book boyfriends are usually better, but I'd still give Ryder a chance."

If only Esme could believe he wanted one. As much as she appreciated Lily's confidence that Ryder wouldn't be able to help falling in love with her, she didn't hold that same faith. That made it even more imperative to guard her heart.

Esme had just gotten both boys fastened into their car seat bases when Ryder texted to ask if she would bring the babies to meet him at the park that bordered Lake Chatelaine near the LC Club.

Her heart fluttered in response. Maybe it was the fact that she'd admitted her feelings for him out loud to Lily—hinted at them, at least—but there was no more denying to herself that she was definitely at risk of being hurt by Ryder Hayes. She tried to tell herself that it was new enough to be only a simple crush. Hormones would be an easy answer, but she suspected it was more than that.

He was attractive and being near him did wild things to her body, yet she enjoyed his company on a much deeper level than physical attraction. Despite how different their backgrounds were, they shared a connection beyond raising kids together.

"No", she said aloud, shaking her head. This was nothing more than a combination of circumstances, his kindness and the gratitude she felt at not being alone any longer.

She thumbed in a reply, agreeing to meet him and offering to pick up carryout from one of the restaurants in town, but he said no, it wasn't necessary. She'd skipped breakfast other than the coffee she'd shared with Freya and Wendell and wanted to believe that the caffeine rush was what made her so tingly as she drove toward the park.

Maybe if she could get the physical need for Ryder out of her system, it would be easier to focus solely on their co-parenting arrangement. That notion of exploring something more with the handsome businessman appealed to her body, although her heart was still skeptical.

Sunshine sparkled off the surface of the lake, and she pulled in next to Ryder's BMW. There was only one other vehicle parked in the lot, although she knew the popular spot would be crowded if the unseasonably warm weather continued through the weekend.

This was her home now, and she felt grateful to be raising her boys in a community that already meant so much to her.

He is your home, a little voice inside her declared as Ryder walked toward her from the edge of the parking lot.

Hayes Enterprises adhered to a casual Friday dress code, so he wore a fine wool sweater in a deep rust color along with dark jeans and Western boots. As per usual, when he smiled, it took her breath away. Esme had a feeling if she polled the women in his office, she'd discover that she wasn't alone in her reaction.

The thought actually made her feel better about her crush, as she was determined to refer to it. Ryder's movie-star features and thick blond hair were universally appealing, so there was no reason to read more into it than necessary.

"How was shopping?" he asked.

"Freya outdid herself once again." Esme put a hand on the car's back door to open it but was suddenly enveloped in a tight embrace.

"Thank you," Ryder said, kissing the top of her head.

She glanced up, confused by the force of his tone. "For meeting you here?"

He bent down and gently kissed her lips. The touch was fleeting, but it ignited tiny fires of need all through her body. "For encouraging me to go back to work. I didn't realize how much I missed having a sense of purpose until I returned to the office." He kissed her again. "But you knew, Esme. You knew I needed it, and I can't thank you enough."

It felt as if he'd tossed a bucket of cold water onto those fires. She appreciated his gratitude but hearing him talk about his purpose and feeling the energy palpably pulsing through him made her understand that being with her and the boys wasn't enough for Ryder.

The knowledge didn't come as a surprise, and she couldn't fault him for it. She was glad to support his happiness, but somehow seeing him so charged after a morning away from her and their sons created a wide gap in their connection.

Taking care of Noah and Chase fulfilled her soul because she was uncomplicated at her core. She'd already been researching recipes for homemade baby food and took so much pleasure in planning her days with the babies, simple as their schedule might be.

What could she offer Ryder that would keep him interested in lackluster, stay-at-home Esme when he probably interacted with so many interesting people doing big things at Hayes Enterprises?

And if his brother was given the CEO position the way Ryder suspected he would be, that would leave him in a position where he was still expected to travel each week for work, wining and dining clients plus hobnobbing with guests at the properties the company managed around the state and beyond, if they expanded the way he'd told her his father planned.

"I'm glad it was a good morning." She kept her tone purposefully light. "I hope the rest of the day goes just as well." There was no doubt the highlight of hers would be the moment when he'd take her in his arms like it was the most natural thing in the world.

"Are you hungry? Because as great as the morning was, I missed…" He gave her an almost bashful smile, which looked out of place on his confident face. "I missed the boys. It's strange not being with them every moment."

"I can't imagine, although I guess I will next year when I go back to work. Freya really did give me the greatest gift making my wish to focus on being a mother come true."

Ryder drew back. "You're amazing, Es. Most women I know would wish for a shopping spree in New York City, not the baby department at Great-Store."

Did that make her amazing or boring? Before Ryder, Esme hadn't given her dream a second thought. In the wake of Seth's cheating, the choice to devote herself completely to being a mother had been an obvious one. But would her late husband have strayed if she'd been enough to keep his attention?

Ryder was more successful and worldly than Seth had ever been. It was ridiculous to think she stood a chance of capturing his attention or affection in any long-term way.

She grabbed the diaper bag and Chase, who was sleeping in his infant carrier, while Ryder hooked Noah's car seat under his arm. He led her toward the grassy area under a cedar pergola that offered a picture-perfect view of the lake.

"I had the restaurant at the club pack a picnic for us. I know my brother came up with the idea, but he's stolen enough of mine over the years that I'm not too concerned. You and I are having lunch al fresco."

"That's sweet of you to plan." Esme tried not to read too much into the gesture. He'd just told her the boys were who he'd missed, which she should appreciate without the ache in her heart. Their arrangement was about parenting together, and this impromptu picnic, plus the fact that he wanted to see Noah and Chase, was proof he took fatherhood seriously.

There was a blanket spread over the grass and an adorable wicker basket that Ryder opened after getting the boys settled. "They don't normally make tater tots on Fridays, but I talked the chef into whipping up an order for us. I know how much you like them."

Esme's stomach growled in response, and Ryder looked quite satisfied with himself as he continued to pull many of her favorite foods out of the basket. There was a turkey sandwich on fluffy brioche bread, a Caesar salad with fresh Parmesan shavings and gorgeous, red, juicy strawberries, which were not easy to come by in the middle of winter.

She was touched by his thoughtfulness and how he'd obviously paid attention during one of their late night conversations, getting to know each other, when he'd quizzed her on the food she liked best.

"The chef kept trying to box up the leftovers from some of the fancy specials on the menu this week." Ryder grinned at her. "But I told him you've got simple taste, so we're going to stick with the basics."

Right. She was basic while he was used to running in circles with women who liked big-city shopping and probably gobbled spoonfuls of foie gras for lunch.

But despite her niggling insecurities, he seemed to enjoy their lunch as much as she did and animatedly shared the plans and ideas he had for the company's future.

They continued to talk, Esme mostly directing the conversation back to Ryder when he asked about her day. No point in highlighting how dull she was by detailing shopping for baby clothes and coffee with two old people.

He placed a hand on her knee, one finger tracing small circles that she felt through the soft fabric of her jeans like he was directly touching her skin. "I'm grateful we're in this together," he said huskily. "There's no way I would have had the mental bandwidth to come back to work with the renewed energy I feel otherwise. When it was just Noah and me, I constantly worried about how to handle my work-load and the expectations, particularly if I needed to keep traveling. Being with you changes everything."

Esme took a small bite of turkey sandwich and nodded. Both Bea and Freya had expressed concern about Ryder coming to view her as a glorified baby-sitter, and she hated to admit that his words gave her trepidation.

Surely that wouldn't be the case when she returned to work. Even though her career as a first-grade teacher wasn't as important or anywhere near as lucrative as his job, she loved teaching and was committed to finding a position at the local school this coming fall.

They'd established ground rules for the babies at their current age and would need to ensure those rules continued to work for both of them as the boys got older. Yet Ryder's hand on her leg felt so good—shockwaves of awareness skittering along her spine—that she longed for more. If she could change the rules to her liking as the boys got older, could she also modify them to accommodate her growing physical attraction to Ryder?

After all, if they were going to be living in such close proximity, with neither of them dating at the moment—and Esme not planning to start anytime soon—what would be the harm in upping their physical connection? She'd just need to keep her heart out of it, which should be manageable. Or would it…?

"What's wrong?" Ryder asked suddenly. "You have a funny look on your face, and you're blushing."

"I think I'm having a reaction to something I ate," she lied, pressing her lips together.

He straightened and gripped her shoulders with his strong hands. "Can you breathe? Is it anaphylactic? Do we need to get you to the hospital?"

Okay, his worry was adorable if unnecessary.

"I'm fine," she said. Then before she lost her nerve she added, "It's really nothing. But I'd feel better if you'd kiss me again."

"Kiss away your allergy?" He stared at her for several seconds and then his mouth curved into a grin.

"Or give me another reason to feel flushed," she suggested with uncharacteristic boldness.

"Why, Miss Fortune, are you asking me to play doctor?"

A nervous giggle bubbled up inside her. "Well, we talked about each other's favorite foods, music and colors, but I guess we never covered our favorite fantasies…"

Ryder sucked in a breath, then leaned in and nipped at her bottom lip. "That's a no-brainer for me. My number one fantasy is anything that involves you." Their mouths melded, and she felt as overwhelmed by the intensity of his words as she did by the kiss. There was no point in pretending she could resist this man. Maybe this was how she'd get him out of her system.

And if nothing else, she'd be left with sweet memories of real-life passion and not just the kind she read about in the pages of her beloved novels. Ryder pulled her closer, lifting her into his lap and then lowering himself to the blanket, taking her with him. She could feel that he wanted her, and that knowledge solidified her decision.

Esme was a grown woman, not a naive schoolgirl unable to discern the difference between physical passion and romantic affection. Why couldn't they be friends with benefits?

It was more than she thought she'd get as a single mother and might be as much as she could handle. She'd given love—or at least commitment—a chance with Seth, and that had been a disaster. As much of a train wreck as her parents' marriage.

Esme had tried to convince herself that in real life she could have the kind of fairy-tale relationship she read about in so many books. But what was the old saying? Fool me once, shame on you. Fool me twice, shame on me.

She'd been fooled by the promise of love both in watching the painful, tension-filled demise of her mom and dad's love story and through her own experience at letting herself fall. Now with their sons to consider, she had to keep her heart guarded. Friends with benefits she could handle. Anything more was too big a risk.

Before things got too out of hand, Noah began fussing, and Esme scrambled off of Ryder.

"Who knew babies made the best chaperones?" Ryder grumbled good-naturedly as he began putting away the leftover food.

"I'm sure you need to get back to the office."

Esme wanted to get physical with this hot, sexy man, but she did *not* want to talk about getting physical. She lifted Noah out of his carrier and moved off the blanket so Ryder could fold it. Chase, bless his heart, had slept through the entire lunch.

"Speaking of that, another reason I wanted to see you all today is because I'm going to be home late tonight. There's a dinner in town with some of the regional management team who have been staying here. Most of them are heading home this weekend, so it's important that I attend."

"Of course," Esme agreed. She turned toward the lake with Noah, hoping her disappointment wasn't written on her face.

"Esme?"

"It's all good."

"Okay," Ryder agreed, taking her free hand in his. "I was just wondering if you'd wait up for me. I'd like a chance to…" He brushed his mouth over her knuckles. "To explore my favorite fantasy when we have more time."

"Oh." She nodded, heat sweeping through her once more. "I can wait up."

"I'm looking forward to it."

"Me, too," she whispered. He'd just never know how much.

Chapter Ten

He was going to murder his brother. Brandon had insisted that after the dinner, the group head over to The Corral, a local bar known for its wings and being the best place in Chatelaine for a game of pool.

It was nearly midnight before Ryder, the evening's designated driver, dropped off the last group of out-of-town Hayes Enterprises' employees at the LC Club, where they were staying. As far as he knew, Brandon was closing down the bar with a couple of cowgirls he'd been flirting with most of the night.

He had finally given up on getting home at a reasonable hour and had texted Esme not to wait for him and that he'd see her in the morning.

A part of him had hoped she'd still be awake, although he knew that wasn't fair.

Taking care of two babies would exhaust even

the most devoted parent, and he had no idea how she managed it each day with a smile on her face. If anyone deserved a few hours of peaceful sleep, it was Esme.

Walking through the dark, quiet house, he reminded himself there was no rush in taking their relationship to the next level. The fact that she wanted to had been a surprise, albeit a pleasant one. He suspected she was still worried about his intentions and whether he was the type of guy to hurt her as her late husband had.

Ryder would never disrespect Esme that way, but he wasn't ready to share how much he cared about her. It made him feel vulnerable, and he hadn't let himself open up like that other than with Steph, which had turned out horribly.

There was too much at risk with Esme. He couldn't imagine his life without her, and not only because she was a better parent than he could ever dream of being. She made him *want* to be better but seemed happy with him just as he was.

With Esme, he didn't have to worry about needless complications or striving to hit some arbitrary expectation. He could completely relax, maybe for the first time in his life. Whether he was happy, sad or in between, she accepted his emotions with the gentle patience she showed their babies. As far as he could tell, nothing rattled Esme Fortune.

She was a gift, a true treasure, which made him wonder at the wisdom of giving in to his desire for her. What if he ended up wanting more than she was willing to give or vice versa? Ryder didn't think he could handle being a parent alone now that he knew how good it felt to share the responsibility with her.

He paused in the upstairs hall and thought about knocking on the closed door to her bedroom. The worry that connecting with her on a deeper, intimate level would come with strings attached, no matter what either of them claimed, might plague him, but deep down he knew that continuing to resist would be a losing battle. He wanted Esme, and when Ryder's mind became set on something, there was no stopping it.

But tonight, he didn't knock. She deserved better than to be roused out of her peaceful sleep. A woman like her was worthy of sonnets and rose petals and…no. He shook his head at his idealistic thoughts, which could only lead to trouble, as he walked into the spare bedroom.

She didn't want those things, not from him anyway. He'd be grateful for whatever scraps of affection she offered and adhere to any guidelines she set for their relationship. He would do whatever it took.

Ryder paused inside the doorway. Something was different. A lamp on the nightstand had been left on, and the sweet scent of vanilla lingered in the air. His heart began to hammer in his chest as he glanced over at the queen bed and saw Esme curled on her side, the sheet and quilt that covered her rising and falling as she breathed.

Was this his imagination playing tricks on him?

As if sensing him, Esme rolled over to face his

direction, her eyes soft and sleepy. "Late night," she murmured.

"Yes," he managed to respond, although speaking around the desire surging through him was difficult.

"I tried to stay awake." She sat up and patted the book on his pillow. "Didn't quite make it."

"But you're here," he observed, like she didn't realize it. "In my room." In his bed.

She inclined her head. "I hope that's okay."

"Yes," he breathed like a prayer.

Her mouth curved into a sensual smile. "Do you want to come to bed?"

He toed off his boots and then started on the buttons of his shirt, his fingers shaking with need. Don't read more into this moment, he counseled himself as he shrugged out of the crisp fabric. It was physical, convenient. They were friends with benefits.

None of it mattered because he wanted her so badly.

"How was your night on the town?" she asked, tucking a dark lock of hair behind one ear.

"Awful." He took the wallet from his back pocket and pulled out a condom, approaching the bed to set them both on the nightstand.

"Really?" Her eyes widened as she tracked his movement. "I've heard The Corral is a lot of fun."

"Nothing is fun without you."

Her smile widened. "That's not true."

"It is for me," he said, then shucked out of his jeans. Wearing only his boxers, he joined her on the bed, the mattress sagging slightly under his weight.

"Then I'm glad you're home."

Home. The word had never sounded so good.

"Are you staying in my bed tonight?" he asked, trying not to growl the question at her.

She seemed to think about her answer—for far too long, in Ryder's opinion. "I was planning on it," she answered and kissed him gently. "If that's okay with you."

He nearly groaned in response but, instead, pulled the sheet off her and then crawled up and over her, placing his knees on either side of her hips. "I'd keep you here forever if I could."

Her green eyes darkened to the color of moss in a shady forest, and he trailed one finger along her jaw and lowered his head.

The kiss was practiced and controlled—that's how it started, anyway. But Esme was so soft and pliant against him, her mouth perfectly fit to his. Soon, he lost himself in the taste of her, feeling reckless and wild. When she grazed her nails over the ridges of his shoulders, it nearly undid him.

He ached for her even though she was right there with him. He yearned for this feeling Esme gave him—not just the physical pleasure of kissing and touching her but the sense that in her arms, he was truly home.

She wore an oversize T-shirt that he efficiently lifted over her head in one movement. Then he was dizzy with the vision of her glorious breasts, which he cupped in his hands as she let out a soft moan. He sucked one pink tip into his mouth, the taste of her like honey, as he caressed the other with his thumb.

"Ryder, I need…" she whispered, her voice strained.

"Me, too, sweetheart," he assured her as he came up for air. "You're beautiful, Esme."

"You're beautiful, too," she answered, and he felt his cheeks heat.

She could make him blush with one simple compliment, but he knew that when Esme said the words, she meant them from the bottom of her heart.

He kissed her again, shifting his weight off her. Then he took his time as his hand moved down her rib cage, her waist and her hips. He hooked one finger in the waistband of her panties and tugged them down. Her vanilla scent mixed with the earthy aroma of a woman, and it once again drove him toward the edge of his control.

She was slick when he touched her, opening for him like she'd been waiting for this moment as much as him. He could have stayed like that all night, kissing and touching her, and been satisfied.

But Esme had other ideas. "Not like this," she said against his mouth. "Together, Ryder. I want to be with you fully. Now."

Her eyes were filled with a mix of passion and determination, and who was he to deny her?

He climbed off the bed, pushed down his boxers, then plucked the condom from the nightstand and sheathed himself.

She lay back on the pillow and stretched her arms above her head, her breasts high and proud and making every last brain cell in his head take a fast train south.

He settled himself over her, then hissed out a breath when her soft hand enveloped his length, guiding him to her center. She surprised him with her assuredness and lack of reserve—a pleasant surprise that made him wish they'd done this sooner.

Then he pushed into her and lost all ability for coherent thought. He filled her completely, and she dug her nails into his back as if she couldn't get enough of him. Which was funny because, at this moment, he intended to give her all that he could.

He thrust in and out, and Esme matched his movements until it was impossible to know where he left off and she began. She moaned—or maybe that was him—and their tongues melded as he drove into her.

"So close," she whimpered after a time, and he could hear the need for release in her voice. Murmuring words of encouragement, he lifted slightly to place his hand between them. Two fingers found that tender spot that sent her over the edge with a strangled cry.

She lifted to bury her face in his neck, then sucked at the base of his throat. It was unexpected enough to make him lose control, and he followed her over, whispering her name as his body trembled in her arms.

"We should have done that sooner," she said, her voice raspy.

"Like the day we met," he agreed, making her laugh. When was the last time he'd laughed with a woman in his bed? He couldn't remember, and the intimacy of it made his chest ache.

When they'd both regained their breath, he rolled off her, took care of the condom in the hall bathroom, then returned to the bed. Esme had the cover tucked up to her chin, and he snuggled behind her, wrapping an arm around her waist.

This felt almost as right as being inside her; only it was a hell of a lot scarier for Ryder since his heart was filled with longing.

"What happened to you?" Bea asked Esme Sunday morning as they perused the shelves inside Remi's Reads. The sisters had met at the bookstore before they were scheduled to join Asa for breakfast.

The three of them did their best to get together for a meal or visit every week, often with Freya or their cousin Camden joining them.

Esme returned the book she held to the shelf and shook her head. "I don't know what you're talking about."

Except she knew exactly what Bea meant. One night—now two—spent in Ryder's arms had changed something inside her. It was as if she'd locked away a part of herself in the wake of Seth's death and learning about his unfaithfulness.

She'd embraced her identity as a mother like that was the only thing that mattered. While she'd rebuilt her life, starting over in Chatelaine, the single-minded focus had centered her and kept her from sinking into sadness and regret.

However, so much had changed since meeting Ryder and Noah. *She*'d changed, but it was too soon to discuss the details with her sister if she could help it.

"Seriously, there's something different about you. You're glowing."

Esme shrugged and waved off the comment. "I picked up a new face scrub at GreatStore last week. I'll text you a picture."

"It's not a new cleanser." Bea sounded suspicious.

"I can't decide what subgenre to choose for my next read. Historical or romantic suspense?" She made a show of glancing at her watch. "I'll think about it and come back later. Asa's going to be waiting for us, and you know how annoyed he gets when he's hungry."

She headed for the front of the store, assuming her sister would follow, then waved to Remi, the bookstore's owner, on her way out.

The door hadn't quite clicked shut when Bea yanked on Esme's arm. "You had sex with him."

She sounded as shocked as an on-the-shelf maiden sister in a historical romance.

Esme tried to look affronted. "You don't know what you're talking about. Who's the one living in fantasyland now?"

She picked up her pace as they approached the diner. If she could get inside, maybe the restaurant would act as a home base. Surely Bea wouldn't discuss something as sensitive as this topic in front of their brother.

Both her siblings had mile-wide protective streaks when it came to Esme, but Asa tended to tease her mercilessly on anything involving real-life romance.

"You slept with Ryder Hayes," Bea insisted.

Esme rarely came close to losing her temper, and she understood the origin of the concern she heard in her sister's voice. But she had no regrets, none that she was willing to hold up to the light of day and truly examine.

She was a grown woman despite being the youngest in her immediate family. Bea and Asa sometimes treated her like the shy, introverted girl she'd once been, but Esme was more than that now. She'd thought she found love with Seth—or at least the family she'd always wanted.

She'd endured heartbreak, betrayal and the terror of wondering how she would support herself and her son as a single mother. On top of that, she'd moved to a new town and made friends, connected with the great-aunt and -uncle she'd never known and then managed to find a way through the unthinkable situation of discovering the child she'd given birth to had been switched for another without her knowledge.

Guilt that she hadn't realized the mistake still knocked around her heart like an unwanted houseguest who had overstayed their welcome.

But despite everything, she kept going, and if this new development in her relationship with Ryder made her happy, she didn't see that it was anyone's business other than theirs.

"For the record, there was very little sleeping involved." She entered the diner and didn't bother to hold open the door for Bea. "And that's all I'm going to say on the matter."

Asa waved from the booth he always chose in the back of the restaurant. The establishment was already standing-room only, and she knew it would get even more crowded once the late sleepers wandered in. The scent of coffee, bacon and thick maple syrup made her stomach growl. Several people she'd met around town—either during her frequent trips to GreatStore or at one of the local parks or trails—said hello.

She liked that Chatelaine was coming to feel like home and didn't want to think about how she'd manage if and when she and Ryder returned to their platonic partnership. She told herself he'd be out of her system by then, but who was she kidding?

"Where are my two favorite babies this morning?" Asa gestured to the high chairs he'd pulled up to the table. "I thought Ryder and the double pack of trouble were joining us."

Esme slid into a chair across from her brother. "That was the plan, but Noah was fussy this morning, so Ryder decided to stay home with them."

Bea took the seat next to Asa and grabbed the carafe of coffee the waitress had left on the table. Although Esme wouldn't have thought it possible to pour coffee aggressively, that was exactly how she would have described her sister's actions.

"I think it's more probable to assume Ryder didn't

want us to read his body language the way I so easily could with our baby sister."

Asa put down the menu and studied Esme. "What
body language?"

"She slept with him," Bea whispered through
clenched teeth.

A throat cleared, and Esme turned, her face on
fire, to see a waitress standing beside the table, order
pad in hand.

"Sorry," Bea muttered, and then each of them
gave their order, although Esme seriously considered storming out of the diner and having a bowl of
cereal back at home.

But the proverbial cat was out of the bag, and if
she didn't have this conversation with her siblings
now, she'd be stuck having it later.

The waitress placed a hand on her shoulder before walking away. "Don't let anyone slut shame you,
girl," she advised.

Esme nodded, then covered her mouth when a
laugh threatened to escape. Asa looked just as amused,
while Bea's cheeks were nearly as red as her hair.

"You heard the woman." Asa nudged their older
sister with his elbow. "Don't shame her."

"I wasn't," Bea insisted. She leaned forward,
palms flat on the table. "I just don't want to see you
hurt, Es. It's clear you like Ryder, but with his family's reputation, you need to be careful."

"What makes you think I'm not?"

Bea frowned. "Well, if he convinced you to—"

"It was *my* idea," Esme interrupted.

"Go, Es," Asa said with a wink.

"I thought you and Ryder were together for the purpose of raising the boys."

"We are." Esme poured herself a cup of coffee and then added two packets of sugar, needing both the caffeine and a small sugar rush. "We're friends."

"That's my kind of friendship." Asa lifted his hand to high-five her, making Esme laugh again.

"I don't want you to get your heart broken," Bea repeated.

Esme knew her sister was telling the truth, and she had a hard time holding on to her anger.

Bea had been the first person Esme called, both when she got the news about Seth's accident and a few days later when she'd been closing out some of his social media profiles and had come across subscriptions to three different dating sites, all very active.

Bea had also been Esme's biggest cheerleader throughout her pregnancy. Despite the waitress's comment, her sister would never shame her. But she needed Bea to respect her decision, even though Esme harbored some of the same concerns deep inside.

"I know, and I appreciate it. I'm not going to jeopardize our partnership for a casual roll in the sheets."

The waitress returned with their meals, darting Esme a pointed look. "Is everything okay here?"

"All good," she assured the stranger, again marveling at life in a small town. While Cave Creek, where they'd grown up, had also been a faded spot on the map, she had never felt like she belonged there the way she did in Chatelaine.

When the woman walked away again, Bea reached across the table and placed her hand on Esme's. "I don't think your feelings for Ryder are casual. That's what worries me."

It worried Esme, too, but before she could answer, Asa chimed in. "Have a little faith in our girl," he counseled Bea. "She might read a lot of romance, but she knows the difference between real life and make-believe."

He forked up a big bite of hash browns, frowning as he chewed. "You do know the difference, right?"

Esme nodded but didn't answer him directly because her throat had gone tight. Knowing and accepting were two different things as far as her heart was concerned.

As usual, Bea seemed to be able to read what Esme was thinking without her saying a word.

"Let's change the subject," her sister suggested. "How are things going with the dude ranch owner?" she asked Asa.

He shrugged. "One step forward and two steps back. We have a meeting at the end of next week, although I heard there's somebody else ready to make an offer on the place. Given all the hoops I've already jumped through, it's hard to believe I have competition. Did you ever want something so badly you knew you'd do whatever it took to have it?"

There was a beat of silence, then Esme and Bea both nodded.

He placed his fork on the plate and leaned back, stretching his arms behind his head. "That's how I feel about this property. I know I'm meant to buy it."

That was how Esme felt about Ryder, unfortunately—like they were meant to be. They were meeting with one of the hospital volunteers later in the week and also had a call scheduled with the doctor who'd delivered both Chase and Noah.

Ryder continued to push for more information about the mysterious volunteer. At the same time, Esme wanted to let the matter go and get on with their lives, although she felt like she'd be doing her boys a disservice by giving up.

She explained her dilemma to Asa and Bea, who also seemed conflicted as to the right course of action.

"Speaking of mysteries," Bea said. "Has anyone heard from Bear yet? The last time I saw Freya, she said he still hasn't responded to her emails or voice messages."

Asa lifted a toast triangle into the air and swooped it around like he was flying a plane. "Our renegade cousin is probably off on some amazing adventure with zero service or cares in the world."

Esme, Bea and Asa hadn't grown up feeling close to Elias Fortune's three grandchildren. Bear, who'd been adopted by their aunt and uncle as a toddler, was the oldest and had always been a free spirit. He'd also made a killing in the oil business.

The middle brother, West, had died a couple of years ago in a shocking accident, but Camden, who at twenty-nine was closest to Esme's age, was more down-to-earth than Bear and had arrived in Chatelaine for the new year. He was as busy as the rest of them, so they hadn't been able to get together as often as Esme would have liked, but they kept tabs on one another.

"I hope Bear's okay," she mused. "It's not like him to go radio silent for so long."

"I'm sure he's fine," Asa said, sounding confident. "He'll no doubt have some incredible stories to share when he finally resurfaces." He polished off the last bite of toast. "And I bet Bear and Ryder will get along. Your guy was telling me about the semester he spent studying abroad in Italy and a few of the other epic trips he's taken."

"What kind of epic trips?" Bea asked as she sipped her coffee.

"Hiking Mount Kilimanjaro and fly fishing in Patagonia were the two that made me the most jealous." Asa's eyes lit with excitement. "Oh, and he visited a dude ranch in Uruguay run by authentic gauchos." He looked at Esme expectantly. "You've probably heard the stories."

"I have." Esme smiled, but it felt strained. Yes, Ryder had shared his travel adventures with her, but hearing her brother talk about them and how Ryder and Bear might connect over their mutual love of adventure brought into sharp focus another difference between her and Ryder.

The farthest she'd ever traveled had been a family vacation to the Grand Canyon, and she'd been carsick half the way from Cave Creek to Arizona.

Ryder was already talking about how to work out a parenting schedule if he had to start traveling again for work. The bulk of his plan involved him taking most of the responsibility for childcare on the weekends, holidays and his vacation time. But what would happen if he developed a case of wanderlust? Or general lust for someone besides her? Esme didn't care to consider either of those options.

They paid the check and then headed out. Esme hadn't wanted to discuss her relationship with Ryder but had to admit she felt a sense of relief that her siblings knew and supported her to the best of their ability.

"If I don't talk to you before you meet with the dude ranch owner, good luck," she told Asa as they said goodbye on the sidewalk. "I'll be sending all my best close-the-deal thoughts your way."

He chucked her on the shoulder. "Thanks, sis. Let's face it, she can't resist my charm forever."

Esme didn't doubt her brother for an instant.

"I do love and support you," Bea said, wrapping her arms around Esme's shoulders for a tight hug.

"She can't help but boss both of us around." Asa enveloped both of them in his embrace. "It's the oldest-child syndrome. She thinks she knows best."

Bea opened her arms to include him in a three-way hug. "I *do* know best. But what I know for sure

Chapter Eleven

"I wish I had more information to give you," Jackie Ashwood, the second volunteer who'd been in the hospital on the labor and delivery floor the night Chase and Noah were born, told Ryder and Esme when they met later that week.

Ryder had suggested they speak with the woman in the Hayes Enterprises' conference room, which offered privacy. Jackie had been accompanied by her granddaughter, who happened to be a labor and delivery nursing assistant who'd also been working that night.

"Is it typical that you wouldn't recognize or already know another volunteer?" Ryder asked. County Hospital wasn't big, and most of the staff he'd talked to before today had known everyone on the floor that night. However, several people had mentioned that Jackie's granddaughter, Ruby, had been a new hire in October.

"That night was chaotic with the storm and flood," Jackie said, sending a sympathetic glance toward Esme. "I'm sure it made giving birth more of an adventure."

"An *adventure* is one way to describe it." Esme's tone was light, but she barely cracked a smile and immediately turned toward the window. She was holding Noah, who'd been particularly fussy for the past couple of days—teething, they both assumed.

Ryder wasn't sure if he'd said or done something wrong, but she'd been distant all morning, her mood directly contrasting with the warm and welcoming woman he shared a bed with at night. They'd been together the past five nights, although it felt like he'd known her forever.

Their bodies fit together like destiny had joined them, and he couldn't imagine anything that would change the way he wanted her.

By unspoken agreement, they didn't talk about this shift in their relationship. It was as if it were too precious for words, which could be misconstrued and dull the power of their connection.

Ruby, the young nursing assistant, stepped closer to Ryder, who was holding Chase in his arms. "What a sweet boy. I bet you love your daddy, don't you?" She cleared her throat and then looked over her shoulder. "You really didn't realize they gave you the wrong baby?" The question was directed at Esme, whose shoulders visibly tensed.

"It was a stressful night," Ryder answered before Esme could. She wasn't the only one who hadn't realized the mistake. "They whisked off the babies as soon as they were born to get their Apgar scores and the initial measurements. We didn't get to hold our sons until the staff brought them back to us. That was nearly a half hour later."

"Yes," the young woman agreed. "I was in charge of weighing the newborns and getting their footprints and measurements."

"Did you put on the ID bracelets?"

"I don't remember that," Ruby said offhandedly, and Ryder felt bad pushing her. She seemed nice enough.

"As Nana said, it was a chaotic night." She held out her hands. "Do you mind if I hold this little sweetie for a minute? I love babies. That's why I chose to work on the labor and delivery floor."

Ryder was slightly surprised at the request and how close the woman stood to him. There was something in the air, a tension he couldn't explain. He wanted to end this meeting prematurely and take Esme in his arms to comfort her however he could, but they might not have another chance to talk to Jackie and her granddaughter. The emails and voice messages he was receiving from the hospital's attorney were becoming more threatening in tone. The powers that be at County Hospital wanted Ryder to drop his unofficial investigation, and he worried they were going to forbid their employees from speaking with him going forward.

Jackie smiled as she watched her granddaughter bounce the baby in her arms. "It's funny," the older woman said. Jackie was heavier set with white-gray hair and the air of a woman who doled out hugs and advice in equal measure. "According to your mama, you never showed much interest in children. She thought you took the job working with babies because of your crush on that single obstetrician."

Ruby made a face. "Mama doesn't know what she's talking about. Sometimes mothers don't have the sense God gave them," she told Chase, like she was imparting great wisdom. "But I'll bet you can always trust your daddy. He's one of the good guys."

Ruby winked at Ryder, and he didn't know how to respond to the compliment, but she didn't seem to need or expect a reply. "I can tell," she cooed to the baby.

If this had been a cartoon, Ryder was reasonably certain he would have seen smoke billowing out of Esme's ears, although he wasn't sure why. The nursing assistant certainly wasn't insinuating Esme was anything less than sensible.

He figured it was a subtle dig at him for how Stephanie had behaved the night of her labor and delivery. Not that he blamed his late girlfriend for her screaming and crying. He'd never given birth, so he didn't have room to talk. But every staff member he'd met with remembered Steph and how vocal she'd been about not wanting to be a mother.

He wondered, as he had several times before now, if she'd changed her mind about sticking around whether the accident would have claimed her life. He highly doubted it, making him sad for Noah and particularly grateful that they both had Esme in their lives.

"If you need anything..." the young nursing assistant told him, leaning forward with Chase in her arms. He hadn't noticed the deep V of her pale pink sweater before that moment but quickly looked away. His gaze crashed into Esme's, and she gave a small shake of her head.

"I think Noah needs his diaper changed," she said tightly. "I'm sure you three can finish up here. Jackie, thank you so much for your time and the ice chips that night."

The older woman beamed. "You remember? I felt bad for you, darlin', because you were alone. Things were such a jumble, and I didn't want you to feel like no one cared."

"Thank you," Esme whispered again, and her voice sounded hoarse with emotion.

Ryder hoped it wasn't sadness. He wanted her to know she would never be alone again. That he would be at her side.

"I have the boys now," she said to Jackie, and Ryder suspected he was not included in that group, which stung. "It was nice to meet you, Ruby. I have a feeling I'll be seeing you again sometime." She darted a pointed look toward Ryder before grabbing the diaper bag from the table and walking out of the room. Trying not to read too much into Esme's parting remark, he asked the women a few more questions before taking Chase back from the nursing assistant. The boy smelled like a bouquet of expensive flowers, which must have been from Ruby's perfume.

Ryder would be bathing his son tonight. Lavender and vanilla were the only scents he wanted to be associated with either of his babies. Like most other staff members he'd talked to, Jackie promised to call if she remembered anything about the other volunteer or additional details that could shed light on who was responsible for the mix-up.

He walked them to the building's entrance, and as he headed back to the conference room, he heard Esme laughing, which did funny things to his heart. He followed the sound to Brandon's office.

Their father was off on another trip, and it was hard to tell whether he was traveling so much in recent weeks in preparation for his retirement or because he was avoiding meeting Esme and Chase.

Brandon had no such qualms and had stopped by her house several times with toys for his nephews.

His younger brother also seemed interested in discussing the goings-on at the company and plans for the future with Ryder. It wasn't pleasant to admit that he couldn't tell whether Brandon was interested in working together or if he would use the information Ryder gave him to get ahead on his own.

Maybe it didn't matter. Ryder wanted the CEO position, but it was nowhere near as important as being a father. He'd deal with whatever his father decided.

"Hey, bro. I changed a diaper." Brandon pumped his fist in the air. "A stinker, too. It turns out I'm a natural. I didn't even mistakenly put it on backward like somebody we know."

"I only did that at the beginning," Ryder said, trying not to feel annoyed. Esme was grinning and looked a hundred times more relaxed and happy sitting in his brother's office than she had with him in the conference room.

"You better be careful," she teased Brandon. "If you get too good at it, I'll put you to work as a babysitter."

"You can call me anytime." Brandon glanced from Esme to Ryder, a startled look flashing over his boyishly handsome features as he took in Ryder's scowl. His brother had the reputation of being irresistible to most women. But after that first lunch where they'd seemed to clear the air, he'd never considered that Brandon would continue to turn his considerable charm on Esme.

Funny how his mood seemed to match hers from earlier, while Brandon had managed to put her in better spirits. They were quite a pair.

"We should go." The words must have come out harsher than he'd intended because her smile faded. She nodded and stood, then picked up a vase of flowers Ryder hadn't noticed sitting on Brandon's desk. "What are those?"

"Your brother got them for me, which was unnecessary but very sweet. Thank you, again."

"Why did you get her flowers?" Ryder knew he sounded like a jerk but couldn't quite stop it.

Brandon shrugged. "It's Valentine's Day. I was buying flowers for all the women in the office. I knew the two of you were going to be here today, so I included Esme in the order. Didn't you give her anything?"

Ryder's face burned. Not only was he a jerk, but he was also an inconsiderate one.

Esme smiled again, but he knew her well enough to recognize that it was forced. "I didn't expect anything," she assured Ryder, then turned to Brandon. "It's not a big deal. He isn't…we aren't…it's complicated."

Brandon guffawed. "Giving flowers to a woman on Valentine's Day is about the least complicated gesture imaginable." He gave Ryder a clear "what the hell, man" look, which Ryder had to admit he deserved.

"How about you babysit for us tonight?" he asked Brandon.

"Ryder, that isn't necessary," Esme protested. "I'm sure your brother has plans."

"Actually, my calendar is completely open for tonight." Brandon placed his palms on the desk and leaned forward, much like their father did when making a point. "I have a rule against dating on Valentine's Day. It gives the wrong impression if you know what I mean."

Ryder knew exactly what his brother meant, which was also why he wouldn't miss the chance to take out Esme.

"Be at the house at seven. We'll get the boys down for bed, so you won't have much to do."

"I can handle whatever you need," Brandon promised.

Esme looked slightly alarmed, and it was a toss-up whether that was in response to the thought of leaving her babies in Brandon's care or the fact that Ryder had asked—well, not exactly asked, but made plans for them to go on a real date.

"But, Ry, even in a one-horse town like Chate-laine, you'll be hard-pressed to get a dinner reservation on Valentine's Day at this late date," Brandon told him. "Unless you're taking her out for popcorn and wings."

"For the record, two horses are often hitched outside The Corral. And I've got a plan."

Esme appeared as surprised by that news as Brandon. "You do?"

He nodded. Not quite yet, but he'd come up with one quickly.

"Then I'll see you at seven," Brandon confirmed.

Esme picked up the flowers Ryder still wished he would have bought her, and they headed for his car.

"I'm sorry I messed up this day," he told her quietly. "I'm going to make it up to you."

"You don't have to do anything. You're not even obligated to go out with me tonight. Ruby seemed nice. I saw her slip you her number during the meeting."

"She did not."

Esme reached forward and pulled a scrap of paper

out of the front pocket of his button-down shirt. "She absolutely did when she took Chase from you."

"I swear to God, I didn't notice. I would have given it back to her if I had. I'm not interested in dating Ruby or anyone."

They'd made it to the car by this point and silently latched the babies into their car seat bases. "Then why did you ask your brother to babysit?"

"I'm not interested in dating anyone but *you*," he clarified.

She stared at him over the roof of the car. "Do you mean that?"

"Esme, do you think I'd sleep with you if I didn't?"

"I thought we were friends with benefits," she said, then ducked into the passenger seat like she didn't want to meet his gaze.

He climbed in and hit the button to start the car but didn't shift it into gear. "We could be more."

"What kind of more are you talking about?"

He pulled out of the LC Club parking lot and glanced at the horizon. The swirling white clouds rolling in from the east seemed to mimic his mood, covering the sky like a thin veil. Esme's question threw him for a loop. It should be simple enough to answer, but nothing felt straightforward to him when it came to matters of the heart.

Ryder didn't want to make promises he couldn't keep and wasn't sure he felt ready to make any vow, not after how Steph had trampled his emotions. Yet deep down he also knew it wasn't fair to compare that relationship with the one he and Esme shared.

Falling for Stephanie had been a dive off a high cliff with nothing but rocks at the bottom to break his landing.

His feelings for Esme were different and more profound, but he didn't know how to trust them or her. While Brandon was the one who took after their father in the obvious ways, Ryder still worried that he had enough Chandler Hayes in him to perpetually mess up his love life—and anyone who made the mistake of falling for him.

"Do we have to put labels on it?" he asked, trying to sound both confident and convincing. "We're already living together and raising our sons. I enjoy being with you, Es, and I'm unsure how I'd manage parenthood alone. Let me take you out on a real date—your rules are fine for co-parenting, but we've been dealing with some big changes in our new reality. Maybe it's time we loosen up and go with the flow."

"You think I need to loosen up?" Her hands were gripped together in her lap, knuckles white from the tight hold. "My late husband also thought I needed to 'loosen up.' Those were the exact words he said to me before he walked out the door that final time."

"It's not a criticism," Ryder assured her, reaching across the middle console to take her hand. "I mean it for both of us. Let's have a little fun. We'll start with one night. It doesn't have to mean anything."

Ryder wished he had a bottle of water in the car so he could wash down his foot, which seemed to be firmly lodged in his mouth.

When he'd proposed marriage to Steph for the sake of their unborn child, she'd accused him of having a heart made of stone. That wasn't true, but every time he let his heart lead, it took him down a dark and dead-end path.

He felt as incompetent at romance as he did at fatherhood and wondered when Esme would realize she could manage both without him. Before this moment, he hadn't given much thought to why he'd never been interested in a long-term commitment with a woman.

There was too much to risk, which went double and triple for a romantic relationship with Esme. If things went south, it could ruin the good thing they had going. Damn, Valentine's Day! He wouldn't be dealing with this dilemma if it weren't for the manufactured holiday.

Her house, which felt more like a home to him than anywhere he'd ever lived, was only a short drive away. As soon as he parked the car, Ryder jumped out and hurried around to the passenger-side door, opening it before she could.

"Esme Fortune, would you go on a date with me?" He placed his hand over his chest, surprised to find his heart beating at an irregular pace. Was he legitimately nervous about asking the woman he lived with, slept with and shared diaper duty with out on a date?

That would be a hell, yes.

She got out and looked at him like he'd lost his mind. "We've already made arrangements for your brother to babysit."

"But we can cancel if this isn't what you want. I want you to want this, Esme." To want *me*, he added silently.

She released a long breath, and it felt like some of the tension of the morning left her body as well. "I'd like to go on a date with you." She offered a shy smile. "Very much."

He leaned in and kissed her, his mind already whirling with ideas. If Ryder could handle anything, it was a plan. "I promise it will be the most memorable Valentine's Day of your life."

Chapter Twelve

Esme took her time getting ready for their date that evening—as much time as the mother of two babies could manage. Chase had been fussy since they'd gotten home from the LC Club—unable to self-soothe and fitfully dozing off in either her or Ryder's arms.

They hadn't wanted to put him down in the crib, where he'd undoubtedly rouse Noah, who was napping like a champ, so they had taken turns trying to comfort him. Ryder thought he'd probably had too much stimulation, and it would take a bit of time before he could relax again, but Esme wondered if he was already protesting his parents leaving him with a sitter for the night.

She hoped it wasn't anything more severe or that the baby was picking up on her anxiety. Perhaps she should have said no to Ryder's offer of something more.

It seemed easy for him not to worry about how their actions today would affect tomorrow's future.

Seth had continually told Esme she needed to lighten up, although she thought she'd gotten over his little digs from their short marriage. Ryder was so kind and complimentary of her ability as a mother, but now she realized that didn't mean he saw her any differently than Seth in other areas.

Still, she wanted this night with him more than she'd wanted anything in a long time, even more than the passion they shared. What if a date could lead to something bigger? It was a risk, and Esme wasn't sure she trusted herself. But proposing the arrangement and that they move in together had also been a leap of faith—one that had paid off more than she could have dreamed.

What would be the harm in blowing off a little steam in the form of a romantic night out? She longed for real romance, particularly because, in the middle of the night, Ryder was everything she wanted in a partner—gentle, loving and attentive to her pleasure.

She couldn't imagine ever tiring of making love with him, but the time they spent managing daily life together was just as precious. It scared her, however, to want more with him. She was afraid of being hurt and then having to put on a brave face for the kids.

But that worry would hold, she reminded herself as she applied a pink gloss to her lips. She adjusted the flowing dress she'd chosen and stared at herself in the bathroom's full-length mirror.

There wasn't much in her closet that felt right for a romantic night on the town, but she loved the muted floral pattern and the way the silky fabric felt against her skin. She'd paired it with a fitted blazer and low-heeled ankle boots and hoped Ryder would notice that she'd made an effort. When she got to the bottom of the stairs, he and Brandon both did a double take, and admiration and desire shone in Ryder's green eyes.

"I can't say much about this guy." Brandon patted Ryder on the shoulder. "But you, Esme Fortune, clean up real nice."

"Thank you," she murmured, heat rising to her cheeks.

Ryder turned to stare at his brother. "How in the world did you get a reputation as a ladies' man when that's the kind of compliment you offer a woman?"

"And you can do better?" Brandon challenged. "You didn't even remember Valentine's Day."

Ryder walked forward until he was directly in front of Esme and then linked their fingers together. "You look so beautiful tonight, sweetheart. If I were a poet, I'd write a sonnet for you. I don't know what I've done to deserve you in my life, but I'm glad we have this evening together."

"If you tell her she completes you, I'm going to barf," Brandon complained.

Esme laughed.

"You look very handsome as well, Ryder. You always do."

He grinned. "Let's get out of here before my numbskull brother realizes exactly what he's signed up for."

Brandon held up the baby monitor. The only noise that came from it was the mobile playing "Rock-a-bye Baby." "Y'all did the hard part. I'm just going to watch a movie and enjoy my own delightful company."

Esme gripped Ryder's hand more tightly. "Are you sure Chase is down? If you think he's going to give Brandon trouble, we don't have to go out tonight."

"Go," Brandon insisted. "You two are giving me a complex like I can't even handle my nephews for a couple of hours."

"We won't be out late," Ryder assured his brother. "The keys to the BMW are on the counter, and their infant carriers are next to the kitchen table."

Brandon frowned. "Do you want me to take them for a ride if they wake up?"

"No, but you need to drive my car in an emergency. You can't just toss them in the back seat of your Porsche. But call us first, no matter what."

"Do all parents worry as much as the two of you?" Brandon looked skeptical.

Esme smiled. She didn't know how to answer that question, but it reminded her how grateful she was to be co-parenting with Ryder. He took the keys to her Subaru, and as they started out of the neighborhood, she tried to figure out their destination.

"I'm guessing you were probably able to get a reservation at the LC Club."

"Nope. Didn't even try."

"Then where?" Esme asked, although she had a feeling he wouldn't tell her quite yet. "I don't think we've covered this, but surprises make me nervous. Giving up control is weird and going with the flow doesn't come easily to me."

His mouth curved into a grin. "Is that so? I wouldn't have guessed that you like being in control." He reached over and squeezed her thigh. "Except when you do that one thing where—"

Esme slapped her hand over his. "You can't talk about that stuff...the stuff we do at night."

He laughed. "I know the *stuff* you're referring to, but why can't I talk about it? It's only the two of us here right now."

She bit her lower lip, embarrassed that she was not only a stick-in-the-mud when it came to surprises but a prudish one at that.

"Hey." Ryder wrapped his hand around hers before she could speak. "It's okay. You don't have to change who you are for me, Esme. Tell me what's going on."

She tried not to fidget as he studied her after parking the car along Main Street, which made her even more curious as to their destination. "Does this still have something to do with that nursing assistant? I had no idea she slipped her number into my pocket."

"I'm sorry," she said automatically. "I'm really trying to go with the flow, but it feels like tonight changes things."

"If you're worried about our co-parenting partnership, I promise nothing will change my commitment to raising our sons together."

"It's not that." Esme shook her head. "I know how to be a mother, Ryder. As silly as it sounds, I was born for that role. But being someone's girlfriend or a romantic partner is different, and I haven't been very successful at it."

She kept her gaze locked on their hands joined in her lap as embarrassment washed through her. "Heck, I don't even own any cute bras. I threw them all away after I learned about Seth's cheating. He wanted me to wear sexy lingerie, and it made me sick to look at the items I'd purchased to live up to some arbitrary standard he set."

"You never told me that." Ryder's tone was gentle.

"Because it's humiliating," she admitted. "You and I are on our first official date, and I'm wearing my boring cotton panties underneath this dress. I know it's easy enough to buy new ones, but even though we've been sleeping together, it hasn't crossed my mind. I buy diapers at GreatStore every week, and they sell nice matching sets of lingerie."

Ryder released her hand and got out of the car. She watched him walk around the front, and then he opened her car door and drew her out. A moment later, she was enveloped in his warm embrace.

"I don't care about fancy underwear. You could be dressed in a potato sack, and I'd still be over-the-moon attracted to you. You have no idea what you do to me."

He used one finger to tip up her chin and gently brushed his mouth across hers. "I don't think this is about lingerie, although once again, your late husband has proved himself to have been aggressively foolish when it came to valuing you. For the record, I'm scared, too."

Esme stared into his vibrant eyes, finding that statement difficult to believe.

"You're an amazing mother. I know I've said it before, but it becomes more apparent every day. We agreed on this arrangement, but you don't need me. Not like I need you."

He tightened his hold and rested his chin on the top of her head, and she wondered at the emotion he was clearly trying to hide from her notice. "Sometimes, I wonder why you keep me around at all," he told her. "That said, we didn't ask for this situation, but I'm not giving up on what we're creating. The men in my family aren't built for lasting relationships. I was determined to be different and change the story after Steph got pregnant. The consequences of that were worse than anything I could have imagined. There's no need for lingerie, Es. You're perfect the way you are. I'm not like you. I'm broken on the inside, and I don't know how to fix it."

Their love could fix it, Esme thought. It was time to admit, at least to herself, that she'd fallen in love with Ryder. She had a feeling he loved her, too, but the heartache of his past made him scared to acknowledge it.

She wanted to tell him what was written on her

heart—to stop pretending. What if they skipped dinner and headed directly to the intimates department at GreatStore? That would be a promising way to spend Valentine's Day.

"Maybe together we can learn to trust again," she suggested softly. They could be the people they yearned to be—for their sons and each other.

She took a step back and looked around, suddenly aware of their surroundings.

"Why are we in front of the bookstore? Remi's Reads isn't open at night."

Ryder's flashed a satisfied smile. "I've become friends with Linc Fortune Maloney, Remi's husband."

"Another one of my cousins," she murmured. "He's Wendell's oldest grandson. Since moving to town last summer, Asa has been close to the Maloneys."

Ryder nodded. "As much as Freya is helping your branch of the family, Wendell outright gifted a large part of his fortune to each of his grandchildren. Linc joined the LC Club, which is how I met him."

"The inheritance is also how he and Remi opened the bookstore." Esme smiled at the cheery facade. "It was a gift to her."

"I can't gift you a bookstore," Ryder said with a soft laugh. "But I've arranged an evening in one. Remi and Linc left the keys under the flower pot next to the front door. We've got the whole place to ourselves."

She gasped, and he quickly added, "I know it's not a traditional Valentine's Day date, but I couldn't think of anything better than spending a quiet evening alone with you."

"Talk about fantasies coming true." She grinned. "As a kid, I dreamed of living in a bookstore."

"Hopefully, the next best thing is having dinner in one."

He led her forward and unlocked the door. Esme's breath caught in her throat as she took in the way the interior of the store had been transformed.

Remi had already put up several cute decorations for Valentine's Day, with paper hearts and red and pink garlands framing several of the tall shelves.

Now a narrow table with a red-and-white checked tablecloth had been positioned in the open area in front of the counter, where tea light candles flickered and the store's overhead lights had been dimmed, lending a truly romantic atmosphere to the space.

She looked at Ryder in wonder. "How did you arrange all this when you were home with me?"

"I had a little help from your sister," he admitted. "Bea also provided the food for the night. I was going to order another picnic from the LC Club, but she offered to make us a lasagna to share."

"My favorite," Esme murmured. "Everything about this night is my favorite. Thank you, Ryder."

He kissed her again. "My pleasure. I don't know if I mentioned my long-standing library fantasy, but…"

She laughed. "I think we can work with that one."

As they sat down at the table, Esme offered him an apologetic smile. "Before we get started, would you mind texting Brandon? I know we've only been gone a short time, but it would put my mind at ease after Chase's fussy day."

Ryder pulled his cell phone from the pocket of his canvas jacket and frowned as he looked at the screen.

"What's wrong?" Esme's heart stuttered in her chest.

"Nothing. It's just strange that I only have one bar of service here, and my phone won't connect to the shop's Wi-Fi. Maybe Remi turns it off at night."

She watched as he typed in a message, then nodded as he glanced up at her. "Looks like it went through."

The phone dinged almost a second later.

"Relax, bro." Ryder read Brandon's incoming text out loud.

Esme blew out a breath. "Good advice from your brother," she agreed. "I'm going to do just that and enjoy this night with you."

The next two hours went by in a flash. They shared the delicious meal Bea had provided, and Esme made a mental note to text her sister *thank you* on the way home. Bea had thought of everything from disposable plates to a bottle of red wine that paired perfectly with the savory meal. There was also garlic bread and a chopped salad dressed with a tangy vinaigrette.

"I know your sister is going to be hiring someone to run the kitchen at the Cowgirl Café," Ryder said as he pushed back from the table after they'd shared a heavenly piece of tiramisu. "But it's obvious that the restaurant business is a calling for her. This is far and away the best meal I've had in a long time,

although your beautiful company might have something to do with it."

Esme smiled softly at the compliment. "Bea's
very talented, and I appreciate you putting so much
thought into this evening."

"Shall we do a little shopping? One other perk for
tonight I forgot to mention is that we have an open
tab, and Remi offered a fifty-percent discount on any
selections we make. It's not flowers, but perhaps we
can assemble a bouquet of books."

He looked so hopeful that Esme felt her heart melt
even more. In between heated kisses, they took turns
reading to each other from random works they drew
from the shelves in various sections around the bookstore. They found books they were particularly interested in and settled onto the comfy couch on the
far wall.

Ryder drew Esme's legs into his lap, and she lay
back against the cushions while he took off her boots
and proceeded to give her the most amazing foot rub.
Truly, the people who had chosen fancy dinners in
crowded restaurants were missing out because this
intimate evening was extraordinary. She'd remember it always.

Ryder checked his phone several times, but with
no incoming texts from Brandon, they lingered in
the bookstore, enjoying the sweet intimacy of their
night. Finally, Esme looked at her watch.

"We should probably go," she said reluctantly.
"I'm sure one of the boys is going to wake soon

enough. I want your brother to have an easy time tonight, so he'll want to babysit again."

She started to put on her boots as Ryder blew out the candles. "Are you saying you'd have a second date with me?"

His teasing tone made her feel giddy. "I think I could be convinced."

After finishing the cleanup, they walked out together, and Esme looked up at the night sky as Ryder relocked the door. The stars were putting on quite a show, but they couldn't compete with how her heart shimmered.

Ryder slipped his hand into hers, but they'd only taken two steps toward the car when his phone began dinging incessantly with incoming texts. A moment later, hers did the same.

"Oh, no," she whispered as she read the barrage of messages.

Ryder cursed. "We must not have had service inside the bookstore after all. I'll call my brother."

They hurried to the car as she tried to process the texts she'd received from both Brandon and Freya. Esme's great-aunt had stopped by the house to drop off a small Valentine's gift for each boy. At the same time, both babies had woken up crying, so Freya offered to stay and help Brandon.

But they'd discovered Chase was running a fever of nearly 103. After a call to the after-hours pediatric line, Brandon headed to County Hospital with the sick boy while Freya watched Noah at home.

"He's going to be fine." Ryder made the pronouncement with confidence, but Esme could hear the panic in his voice. He dialed his brother's number, but Brandon didn't pick up. After a terse message, Ryder disconnected.

"I'll call Freya," Esme said, already dialing the number. Her great-aunt sounded frazzled but insisted that Esme and Ryder go immediately to the hospital. Bea was already on her way to the house to relieve Freya, which comforted Esme, but she could hear Noah whimpering in the background.

"Are you sure he doesn't have a fever? Should he have gone with Chase?" As scared as she'd been the first time they put Chase in her arms, she'd never known terror akin to what she felt now.

"He's fine, and a hospital is no place for a healthy baby," Freya answered. "We'll manage until you bring that boy home."

Esme ended the call but continued to hold the phone with trembling fingers.

"He's going to be fine," Ryder repeated. She nodded and murmured her agreement, wishing the doubts weren't piling up in her mind like mounds of dirty laundry. The amount of fear she felt was nearly matched by guilt.

"If I'd been there, maybe I would have realized he was too warm. They are too young for us to leave them. What was I thinking?"

Ryder made a noise low in his throat. "Are you saying I was too intent on a child-free night that I put my son at risk? Is that what you believe?"

The intensity of his voice shocked her.

"I didn't say that, and I don't think it. He's not just your son—he's *our* son. We both chose to leave him with your brother during our date." She squeezed the phone so hard it was surprising the device didn't crack in her hand. "We made a terrible mistake."

Chapter Thirteen

Two hours later, Ryder's stomach still churned as he watched one of his precious baby boys asleep in the hospital bassinet. It had been a chaotic arrival, mainly because the hospital staff had assumed Brandon was the father, so it took time for them to fix the paperwork and allow Esme and Ryder back to his room.

Was this hospital always so incompetent in identifying people?

Brandon had immediately transferred Chase into Esme's arms, and the three of them awaited the results of the blood tests. Finally, the doctor returned and explained that Chase was suffering from a bacterial infection he felt confident could be treated with rest and IV antibiotics.

Brandon had appeared stricken and apologized profusely, although Ryder knew it wasn't his brother's fault. Esme said the blame lay with the two of them, but she had to know he deserved the lion's share of the responsibility. He'd been the last person to hold Chase before his fever spiked, and he couldn't help but wonder if he'd missed something.

After answering a litany of questions from the attending nurse, Ryder had sent Brandon home with assurances that he'd done nothing wrong.

He and Esme had followed the nurse as she pushed the wheeled bassinet down the hall and then rode the elevator to the floor above where their baby would be spending the night.

Now they watched the boy, who appeared to be resting comfortably. Ryder had never hated something more than he did the thought of his sweet son hurting. Esme eventually got up from the chair she sat in to stand next to the crib.

"Hush, little baby," she began to sing, and tears sprang to Ryder's eyes. No one had told him about the pain he would feel when one of his children was sick. He would have done anything—made any promise—to take the child's suffering into his own body, but that wasn't an option.

He felt incapable of knowing what to do or how to comfort Chase or even Esme. She continued to sing, stroking the baby's soft cheek. Even under the weight of worry, she knew how to handle the situation. She was so much better than Ryder in every way.

Esme turned as a different nurse walked into the room. "Visiting hours are almost over," she said, her gaze traveling from Esme to Ryder.

Esme gripped the side of the bassinet. "I'm not leaving my son."

"Hospital policy only allows one parent to stay overnight with a minor."

"He's three months old," Ryder explained. "There has to be a special exception for babies."

"I'm sorry, but no there isn't." The woman looked sympathetic but resolute in sticking to the rules. "I'll give you a few minutes alone to decide."

A heavy silence filled the room, and although it killed Ryder to think about leaving his son, he knew the right decision.

"You'll stay," he said after a moment.

"Yes, I think that's best," Esme agreed, her gaze on Chase. "I'll text you any updates. Would you please let me know if Noah is okay when you get home? I can't stop worrying about him, too."

Was she so quick to dismiss Ryder because she didn't think he could handle the responsibility of keeping vigil with their sick child? Or because this awful night had shown her what he already knew— she didn't need him the way he did her.

Unwilling to consider either option, he rubbed his chest, which ached like it was splitting apart. Maybe she'd been right in her reluctance to take their relationship to the next level. Emotions complicated everything, as Ryder knew from past experience.

"I'll text you right away." He stepped toward her, but she backed up like she couldn't stand to be touched by him at this moment. Clearly, she blamed him for what happened as much as he blamed himself.

Another jab straight to his heart.

"I'll be here in the morning," he told her and then bent down to give Chase a kiss on the forehead. The baby slept soundly and didn't feel as hot to the touch, which Ryder hoped meant he'd taken a positive turn.

"Bring Noah," Esme said. "Please. If he's still well, and the doctor believes he's in the clear, I think it will help Chase to have his brother close by."

"You consider them brothers?" Ryder didn't know why the comment shocked him.

"Don't you?"

"I do, yes."

The whole point of their arrangement was to raise the babies together and not just for Ryder and Esme's benefit. He'd thought a thousand times about what he'd do differently from how his parents had treated him and Brandon. Of course, Chase and Noah would grow up as brothers. If Ryder had learned one thing from this situation, it was that sharing DNA was not the only way a family could be created.

Esme, Chase and Noah were his family now.

"Noah and I will see the two of you as soon as visiting hours begin in the morning. Good night, Esme."

He didn't want to leave without holding her, but as if she could read his mind, she crossed her arms over her chest and gave a slight shake of her head.

"Good night, Ryder."

He walked out into the night, amazed at how a few hours could change everything. It felt like their date in the bookshop had been something he'd imagined instead of real life.

The stars twinkling above them hours earlier had been blotted out as thick clouds filled the sky. He did his best to ignore the tight worry that held him in its grip. There was no way he would risk losing Esme and their partnership now.

He couldn't bring himself to define the emotions swirling through him but refused to let this night pull them apart. As he drove through the quiet streets of Chatelaine, his mind searched for ideas of how to make sure he kept his family together—forever.

Esme's neck and heart ached in equal measure the following morning after a night spent in an uncomfortable chair, although Chase was thankfully being discharged. After a course of IV antibiotics and fluids, the baby improved rapidly through the night.

He'd already had his first feeding that morning and offered a gummy smile to every nurse who came in to check his vitals. Ryder had also reported that Noah was completely healthy. Esme counted on him staying that way—her heart couldn't take the stress of another night like the one she'd just endured.

What made it worse was knowing that from now on, she'd have to deal with these sorts of issues on her own. Not completely, of course. She knew Ryder would be there for whatever she or their sons needed, but Esme couldn't keep pretending.

She'd fallen for him, even though she'd promised herself she was done with love after Seth. Knowing that one of their babies had gotten sick on a night when Esme and Ryder had left the boys with a sitter felt like a sign. She could not be distracted or allow her focus on being a good mother to be derailed.

Ryder clearly cared for her, but she was too afraid of being truly hurt to let him in.

If Esme were going to take another chance on opening her heart, it would be to someone willing to risk that fall in return. Maybe once she told Ryder how she felt, he would open up, but she wasn't counting on it.

"Who am I kidding?" she asked Chase as she lifted him into her arms. She couldn't help hoping and praying that Ryder would love her in return. Esme had spent most of her life immersing herself in fairy tales and love stories. Was it so wrong to want one of her own? Sadly, yes if the fairy tale turned into a nightmare, as it had in her family growing up and with Seth.

The baby didn't appear to have an answer for her but snuggled more closely into the crook of her neck. She wanted both her sons to grow up in a happy home. There were too many memories of her parents fighting and their petty little wars of words, plus the affairs and backstabbing that had been so prevalent throughout her childhood.

Ryder had been nothing but kind, but she still didn't know how to trust herself enough to trust him. It was safe enough to raise kids together, but she knew how being raised in a house filled with tension and animosity could impact a child.

Asa and Bea had done their best to protect Esme from the worst of it, and before becoming a mother, she would have claimed not to have been affected by the rancor that had filled her childhood home. But now, she wasn't only making choices for herself. Her decisions would have consequences for her children, and they deserved to see their parents content. She could be happy with Ryder if only she could trust him enough to give them a chance.

As the door to Chase's room opened, she expected to see Ryder enter. Instead, Freya walked in. Her great-aunt carried a giant stuffed bear with a blue bow tie around his neck.

Esme smiled and gestured her forward. "Good morning. I didn't expect to see you here."

Color stained Freya's cheeks. "I didn't expect to be here," the older woman admitted. "But I wanted to check on the baby and also see how you're doing after sleeping in a hospital room chair."

Esme wrapped her arms around the older woman. "I'm so glad you stopped by."

Freya was stiff for a few moments and then seemed to relax into the hug. It was clear that Elias's widow cared about Esme, her siblings and her cousins. Esme wanted to believe that as time passed, she'd continue to feel more comfortable about her role in each of their lives.

"My neck has seen better days." She rubbed the back of it with her free hand. "Would you like to hold him for a few minutes?"

"Oh, I'm sure he's happy in his mother's arms," Freya said.

"He'll be just as happy in yours," Esme promised. She took the bear from the older woman and placed it in the bassinet, then gave Chase to Freya.

Freya's expression gentled as she glanced down at the baby. "It's still difficult to believe that the mix-up happened and nobody caught it." Her gaze sharpened on Esme. "Have you and Ryder discovered anything more?"

She shook her head. "No, but I'm not sure he's ready to give up the search. I wish I didn't feel like I should have been the one to realize it. How could I not recognize my own baby even with all the trauma and chaos surrounding that night?"

Freya traced a finger over the cleft in Chase's chin—the one he'd inherited from his father. "Love makes us see what we want to, even if it's not always the full breadth of the matter."

"That's true, and I trusted the staff at the hospital to get things right."

"Of course, you did," Freya agreed.

"Once again, I can't thank you enough. If you hadn't gifted me that DNA test, I'm not sure when or if we would have realized the switch happened. It's like I needed you to discover the truth. You truly are a gift in our lives, Freya."

Her great-aunt looked uncomfortable at the compliment. "I don't think you should give me all that much credit. I barely did a thing."

"But what you did changed my whole life," Esme assured her.

The woman's eyes widened in shock, but before she could answer, the door opened again.

"Hi." Ruby Ashwood, the young nursing assistant, popped her head into the room. "I heard one of your babies spent the night here."

Esme moved to stand behind the giant teddy bear propped up in the bassinet, feeling like she needed a shield between herself and the woman who'd so blatantly flirted with Ryder during their meeting.

"Ryder isn't here," she said, noticing that Freya gave her a funny look. "He's coming soon with Noah."

"Okay." Ruby nodded and stepped into the room. "How's that little guy?" She gestured toward Chase.

"On the mend, thankfully. You'll be relieved to know I spent the night with him because he's my priority."

"I know my comment came out badly." Ruby scrunched up her adorable button nose. "I don't have a great relationship with my mom, and I tend to project that on everyone else. I'm sorry." She blew out a breath. "My grandma raked me over the coals for making you feel bad, if that helps."

Esme thought about it and then offered Ruby a smile. "I suppose it does."

"The younger generation should listen to their elders," Freya murmured to Chase, although it was clear who the comment was meant for.

Ruby grinned at the older woman. "You must be Chase's grandma."

"No. I'm Freya Fortune. I'm…"

"His great-great-aunt," Esme explained. "Freya is the reason my siblings and I moved to Chatelaine."

Ruby whistled and grimaced slightly. "You must be really special. I don't know anyone who wants to come *to* this town, although I suppose things are getting better thanks to all the Fortunes moving here. But this place is still about as tiny as they come."

Esme laughed. "You haven't visited my hometown of Cave Creek."

"Can't say that I have," Ruby agreed.

"Chatelaine is a wonderful town," Freya insisted. "And a great place to raise a family." She quickly glanced at Esme. "At least, that's what I've heard."

"I suppose." Ruby nodded. "My family has been here for generations. My great-uncle Joe died when that mine collapsed years ago. It took a toll on the whole town, almost like everyone was frozen in time, so it's nice to see new restaurants and shops opening."

"Like Remi's Reads," Esme supplied, still touched by the special evening Ryder had given her before everything had gone horribly awry.

"And your sister's restaurant," Freya added.

"The Cowgirl Café," Esme told Ruby. "You'll have to check it out when Bea has her grand opening in a couple of months."

"I will. Hey, Esme, no hard feelings about me giving my number to Ryder, right? It wasn't cool, I know, and not just because Nana lit me up. For the record, he never called."

Esme accepted the woman's apology without mentioning that she'd been the one to throw away the slip of paper.

"You look familiar," Ruby said to Freya, inclining her head as she studied the woman. "Have we met?"

"No," Freya answered definitively.

"She visited me in the hospital after Chase was born." Esme stepped out from behind the teddy bear and moved closer to her great-aunt, who seemed taken aback by Ruby's question. "You probably saw her then."

"Probably," the nursing assistant agreed. "Well, I've got to get back to the L and D unit. See you around, Esme. Nice to meet you, Freya Fortune."

"That girl was odd." Freya transferred Chase back to Esme's arms. "I don't think she's ever seen me before."

"Maybe you have a familiar face," Esme suggested.

Ryder walked in with Noah at that moment, and Freya made an excuse to leave almost immediately.

"Is she okay?" Ryder asked when it was just the two of them and the boys in the room.

"I think so." Esme's heart stuttered as Ryder studied her, then warmed as Noah wriggled in his carrier at the sound of her voice. She had about as much control over her heart as she did her tingling body where Ryder was concerned.

"Want to trade babies?" Ryder asked.

Esme gasped.

"I didn't mean it like that," he amended. "I'd like to hold Chase if that's okay?"

"Of course it is." She shook off the shock of his question. Something about the visit with Freya and Ruby had put her on edge even more than before.

"The nurse said she'd be in to finish his discharge papers within the next half hour."

"You had us worried, buddy." Ryder kissed Chase's forehead, then glanced up at Esme. "How are you doing?"

"I'm okay now that I know both of our boys are good. I'm also ready to go home and don't want anything like last night ever to happen again."

"We'll do our best to make sure it never does," he told her, even though she knew it was a promise he could not keep. "But no matter what, we'll get through it together."

"I'm sorry about last night. I was upset and had no right to take it out on you."

Esme had spent most of the night thinking about exactly that—her and Ryder together and what it meant for their future and that of their sons. There were no guarantees, but she also knew Chase and Noah had to be her number one priority, especially since she and Ryder had committed nothing to each other. It could impact the boys if she got too invested in their shared connection, and he lost interest.

She wished she had enough faith in herself to believe she was enough for him. They'd both been hurt by love and had a hard time trusting. That was undeniable, but Esme wanted more.

Even though she'd done her best not to have expectations or to put labels on their relationship, she loved Ryder Hayes with all of her heart. And if they kept on this path and her feelings weren't reciprocated, her heart could be shattered into a million pieces.

"I need to tell you something, Ryder." She looked around the sterile hospital room that had become so familiar to her in the last twelve hours. "Maybe I should wait, but I don't want to. I need to say it."

He nodded like he could read her mind. "I don't want to wait, either, Esme. I have something I need to tell you as well."

She couldn't decipher the mix of emotions in his green eyes, but was it too much to hope they had the same idea in mind? Should she wait and let him say it first?

No. She was ready to take this risk, and she didn't want him to think she was only doing it in response to his declaration. He needed to know it came from her soul.

"On the count of three, we say it together."

He looked slightly confused by her request but nodded.

"One, two, three," she counted, then drew in a breath and said, "I love you."

At the same time, he said, "We should get married."

It felt like a grenade went off inside her, shrapnel flying everywhere as she tried to make sense of his statement. While his words should've been a dream come true, something about his tone suggested he didn't feel the same way as her.

But before either of them could say anything more or respond to the other, the nurse walked into the room to discharge Chase.

Chapter Fourteen

Ryder wasn't sure he could have misread the situation with Esme more if he'd tried.

He sat on the sofa in their living room—her living room, technically—and stared straight ahead, unable to wrap his mind around the three little words she'd said to him.

I love you.

He'd honestly thought he had the perfect solution worked out for the two of them. Marriage would tie them together forever. Of course, he knew that plenty of marriages ended in divorce. His parents' bitter battle had been one for the ages.

But he was proposing they officially join their lives for entirely sensible reasons, taking out the complicated emotions that often sent couples spiraling. They wouldn't grow apart or fall out of love because, as he saw it, getting married was simply taking their practical arrangement to another level.

His idea would keep both of their hearts safe. He thought Esme understood that he couldn't let himself love again, but those three words and the look of hope in her eyes told a different story.

Neither of them had spoken on the way home about what they'd each said in the hospital room, and she'd immediately gone upstairs to put the boys down for a nap.

He thought they could just pretend none of this had happened, then cursed himself for being ten kinds of a fool. There was no pretending, but Esme might understand if he could figure out a way to explain it.

He looked up as she descended the stairs, but instead of sitting next to him as was their custom, she chose the chair opposite the sofa. It wasn't as if they were that far apart, but to Ryder, it felt like an ocean between them.

Esme pulled her legs up, tucked them underneath her, then crossed her arms over her chest. "We need to talk about what we said at the hospital."

Rewind, a voice inside his head begged. *Do over. Forget any of it happened.* Ryder ignored that voice.

"I proposed marriage," he said, like she didn't remember.

"I told you I loved you," she countered, her voice strained.

"You can't. You shouldn't."

"I do." She uncrossed her arms and placed her

hands on the arms of the chair, leaning forward. "And I think you love me, too."

For a moment, he couldn't breathe. "Marriage will solve our problems." It felt easier to ignore her statement, which couldn't be true. Not when he'd made the decision not to love again. Even his love for Chase and Noah terrified him, especially after Chase's health scare.

But kids were different. They were loyal to their parents, even when mistakes were made over and over. Ryder's family was proof positive of that.

Loving Esme would make him vulnerable in a way he couldn't comprehend.

"I don't think so," she said softly. "I spent most of my life dealing with my parents' unhappy marriage. By the end, they could barely tolerate each other, yet they refused to walk away. They certainly weren't in love anymore."

"Exactly." He nodded. "We're not going to bother with love."

She sniffed. "Is love such a bother?"

"You know it is. We both do. My parents hurt each other, too, and I swore I'd never do that to myself or someone else. But they did love each other at the start, which made it so much worse when things went bad. I heard my mom crying in her room when Dad didn't come home, and it broke my little-kid heart. If she hadn't loved him, maybe his betrayals wouldn't have hurt so much." He let out a deep breath. "And when I found out Steph was pregnant, I threw myself into loving her. Turned out it was more like falling on a bed of nails. Maybe she wouldn't have felt so trapped if I hadn't expected more from her. Without the pressure she felt, breaking free wouldn't have seemed so necessary."

Esme shook her head. "You can't blame yourself for Stephanie's death. We've talked about that, Ryder. You didn't force her into that car. I know you would have given her whatever space or support she needed."

He pressed his lips together and didn't respond. The rational side of his brain wanted to believe her, but it was hard to release the guilt that had lodged in his heart.

Esme studied him. "We can't pretend we have no feelings for each other."

"I don't want to pretend. I… I care about you, Esme. You're a great mom and a wonderful co-parenting partner. We get along great in everyday life and…" He glanced at the ceiling. "And at night. We've got a good thing going. There's no reason to mess it up with unnecessary labels."

Esme stared at him for several seconds, her greenish-gray eyes flashing like sparks danced inside them. "You don't think becoming husband and wife is a label? Because I've been in that kind of marriage, Ryder, and it almost broke me."

"This is different," he insisted. "We understand each other."

"Yes." She blinked as if to bank the fires burning in her gaze. "I think we do."

"This conversation is not going the way I wanted

it to." Frustration pounded through him. "Can we go back to how things were last night, Esme? Before Chase—"

"We can't go back, and maybe we should have never started down this path in the first place."

The lack of emotion in her voice made his heart clench. Wasn't this what he'd feared in the first place—that she'd come to realize she never truly needed him?

"What are you saying?" he forced himself to ask. "Have you changed your mind about raising the boys together? Are you giving me some kind of ultimatum?"

It was a ridiculous accusation to lob at her. Still, memories flooded his brain of the times his father had complained about his mom and claimed that if she hadn't made so many demands, he wouldn't have been forced to repeatedly disappoint her.

Ryder didn't want to fail Esme, but clearly he already had.

"I would never jeopardize Chase's and Noah's happiness for my own benefit," she said with preternatural calm. "I hope you know that."

He nodded vigorously. "I do. I trust you." Ryder reminded himself they did not have the same toxic relationship as his parents. He and Esme would be able to work things out, provided they were both on the same page. "I just want—"

She held up a hand. "You've made it clear what you want, as well as the limits of what you can give. I'm willing to honor that for the sake of our sons."

The vise in his chest loosened slightly. "You won't regret marrying me," he assured her.

"I'm not talking about marriage. I married Seth believing I could make him love me if I tried hard enough. But that's not how love should work, Ryder. It needs to be freely given. I fell in love with you. It's not your fault. I didn't even mean it to happen, and like you said, I'm sure I'll get over it eventually, but not with how things are now. This house…"

She shook her head. "I think you need to move back to your apartment for the time being. You were right. We need to find a property that will allow us to live together but give each of us more privacy. The investigation into who was responsible for Chase and Noah being switched has taken priority, but I'm sure we can find something that will work for both of our needs."

Ryder wanted to tell her this house worked, even though buying a different one had been his idea. He needed Esme not to give up on him. "I don't understand. Everything was so good—"

"Was it?" She laughed without humor. "I suppose I thought so, too, but I believed the same thing when Seth and I got married. I guess that makes me the fool."

"You aren't a fool."

"Maybe I'm just a woman who isn't worth taking a risk to love." Her voice cracked on the last word, nearly gutting Ryder.

He didn't want to hurt Esme, yet he could see the tears shimmering in her beautiful eyes. He hadn't wanted things with Steph to go as badly as they did, yet he hadn't been able to stop that either.

Maybe he was cursed in a different way than his father and brother. Maybe his inability to love someone in the right way made him just as toxic as the other men in his family.

"Do you want me to go now?" As awful as this conversation was and the fallout from it would be, he still didn't want to leave her. She called herself a fool, but he was the bigger idiot.

"It's best for now. I think we both need a little time. But I don't want to keep you from either of the boys. We'll figure out how to successfully co-parent without having a romantic relationship. Come back around dinnertime," she told him. "Bea brought over a few meals for the freezer, so we can have dinner as a fam… We can have dinner together."

"If that's how you want it." He couldn't keep the disappointment from his gaze, so he didn't try.

"It isn't how I want it." She swiped a hand across her cheeks. "I told you I love you, Ryder. I want more than this. It's stupid and naive, but—"

"You want the fairy tale."

"No. I want real life, and I also want a true partnership. I want somebody brave enough to love me in return through the good times, laughter and moments like last night that frighten the heck out of us. I want passion and to butt heads and not to strive to meet some arbitrary standards I don't even understand."

She nodded as if willing him to be the man she needed. "But I don't want convenience. I won't settle for less than what I deserve. At the end of the day, my sons need to see their mother happy. Being with you has been wonderful for so many reasons, but a marriage of convenience isn't enough."

Unfortunately, it was all Ryder had to offer her.

He stood, his entire body itching to take her into his arms. Yet he didn't touch her. He had no right to anymore. "I'll see you later. Call or text if you need anything."

The smile she gave him broke his heart all over again. "I wish you were willing to give me what I need."

"I do, too," he agreed and walked away.

"I'm going to *kill* him," Bea said the following morning as they walked along the path that circled Lake Chatelaine. "It's going to be slow and painful."

Esme adjusted her grip on the double stroller's handle and glanced over the top to make sure both boys were still content and cozy, bundled in blankets and protected from the wind by a plastic cover. "You can't kill him. He's the father of my babies."

"One of them." Anger darkened Bea's voice.

"Don't say that." Esme shook her head. "Would you want someone to suggest that I'm not Chase's real mom? Ryder is Noah's father, and no matter what happens between us, that won't change."

"I know." Bea let out a sigh. "I'm sorry. My comment was uncalled for. I know the babies belong to both of you, but seeing you hurt makes me so upset."

"It's my own fault." Esme hated to admit it, but

she couldn't deny the truth. "Ryder and I made a deal. We were going to be friends and co-parents. I had rules, and I broke the unspoken one. The most important rule, as it turned out." The cold wind whipped up from the lake as if chastising her for her weakness.

"He broke the rules as much as you."

Esme appreciated her sister's loyalty but only had herself to blame for her broken heart. "I fell in love with him. I didn't mean to—it happened effortlessly, which I thought changed the rules."

"You were happy with him. He's a good father. Plus, you went through something traumatic together. Not many people can say they started a relationship because their babies were switched at birth."

"That's the whole point." Esme paused for a moment and looked up toward the pale blue sky. She needed to get a hold of her emotions. It wouldn't do her or the babies any good if she continued to be so undone by her feelings for Ryder.

"I was the one who suggested our arrangement. I came up with the rules. He didn't need them because he wasn't going to fall in love with me."

Bea placed a hand on Esme's arm. "You don't believe that. You told me you think he loves you. You said you told him that."

"Doesn't that make me an even bigger fool? Even if he feels something more, he's smart enough to focus on the boys."

"He proposed marriage to you. Marrying somebody you don't love is *not* smart. Our parents were proof of that. If he loves you, he needs to man up and admit it."

"It's too late," Esme said sadly and began walking again. Moving kept her from wallowing in her sadness. "Now I'd think he was just saying it to appease me. I don't want to be handled, Bea."

It would be difficult to be near Ryder and accept that their relationship would not be the same as it had been before. But if she focused on the practical aspects of caring for the babies, it made their long future together seem slightly more bearable.

"We're going to look at properties at the end of the week. There are a couple that have main houses plus a guest house. One is a ranch house in the gated community with two primary suites with private entrances." She took a steadying breath, then added, "So if he brings someone home…"

"If Ryder Hayes brings a woman home to spend the night in the house he's sharing with the woman raising his kids, then he is not the man I believe him to be."

Esme frowned. "You're the one who warned me about the Hayes men. Why would it come as a surprise to you?"

"Because I've seen the way that man looks at you. It is not the look of a guy who wants to date other women."

"I can't let myself think like that. You and Asa warned me for years about believing the stories I read in books. Maybe I should have paid more attention."

"You are the hopeful Fortune." Bea placed an arm

around Esme's shoulder. "And there's no one more deserving of a happily-ever-after than you. I'm sorry that Ryder is too scared or chicken to give it to you, but I don't want you to stop believing."

How could Esme keep believing when each time she did, it left her with a broken heart? She'd been angry after discovering Seth's betrayal, but her sadness from ending things with Ryder was more profound. The loss of him felt woven into her DNA.

"Do you remember when I was eight years old and fell out of the tree, and the branch got lodged in my arm?"

"Yes, like it was yesterday." Bea sounded surprised at the sudden change in topic. "It's when we realized Dad was afraid of blood. You came in with that thing sticking out of the back of your body, and he nearly passed out."

"Mom and Dad were good at making things about them."

Bea smiled. "That's a nice way to put it."

"You bandaged me up," Esme reminded her. "I still have a scar. Because it's on the back of my arm, I don't often notice it. Sometimes out of habit, I run my finger along the ridge. I feel like that's what my heartache from Ryder will become—a scar that's always with me. I kind of hope so." She sighed wistfully. "I remember the pain of that fall, but I also remember your sweetness in that moment. I want to think about the sweet times I shared with Ryder. I don't want to hold on to the sorrow or bitterness at what could have been. That doesn't do Chase and Noah any good."

"You are one of the best people I know," Bea told her, admiration and deep affection glittering in her eyes.

"For years, you thought I was just a twerpy little kid," Esme said with a laugh. "We also have Chatelaine to thank for bringing us closer together."

"Do you think we owe any of that thanks to Edgar and Elias?" Bea asked.

"Not at all. Even I'm not *that* generous."

They both laughed. "Speaking of which, I saw Wendell in the diner the other day," Bea told her. "He and Freya were talking about mystery miner number fifty-one. He really thinks that note on the back of the castle was more than just someone stirring up trouble. Freya seemed pretty bothered by the possibility."

"The same thing happened when I talked to them about it. I don't like to think about anything upsetting her," Esme said, "but I understand. She knows her husband holds some responsibility for fifty deaths, and maybe the thought of one more being added to the count is too much."

"That's understandable," Bea agreed. "I wish she didn't feel responsible for making reparations. She was nowhere near Chatelaine when everything happened at the mine."

"I think as much as Freya is helping us, we're also helping her."

Bea looked skeptical. "By spending Uncle Elias's money so she doesn't have to?"

"No, silly." Esme rolled her eyes. "It's not about the money."

"Then what is it about?"

"We're helping her let go of the past and move forward. It's what I tried to do by taking the risk of telling Ryder I loved him. Too bad it didn't work out for me."

"I think it's working out for Freya," Bea said. "If that makes you feel any better."

Esme thought about that and then nodded. "Despite having my heart broken all over again, I don't regret any of the choices I made with Ryder."

"You'd sleep with him all over again?" her sister asked.

"Oh, I definitely don't regret that."

Bea chuckled. "And you think you can stay platonic with him?"

"I have to," Esme said with a sigh. "Whether he truly loves me and is too afraid to admit it, or his heart was irreparably damaged by his past hurt, I guess I'll never know. But I'm going to do what's right for my babies."

"Let's plan a trip to Remi's Reads soon," Bea suggested. "I think you're going to have a lot of long nights to fill."

Esme groaned and then hugged her sister. "That's the truth."

their babies a lullaby, either his favorite Bruce selections or the classics she was teaching him.

Although she invited him to dinner each night, it wasn't the same. She usually had some excuse for not eating with him and suggested they take turns handling bedtime for Chase and Noah.

Ryder felt as though he were the one being handled, and he didn't like it one bit. But he kept a smile on his face when he was with her because the alternative of navigating the change in their relationship seemed to be fully disengaging and dividing their time with the boys.

That was the worst thing he could imagine, not just because of his own experience as a child of divorce. He didn't want to lose the connection he and Esme shared, even though it felt as though the future he wanted was slipping through his fingers.

A knock at the door startled him. It was almost ten in the morning, but he'd called the office earlier to say he was working from home. He hadn't told anyone that he and Esme were now living apart. It would have to come out sooner than later, but he didn't want to see pity or disappointment in the eyes of the people who knew him best. And pretending that everything was okay for the past few days at the office had been excruciating, which was why the work-from-home scenario seemed a viable option.

He got up from the small desk that sat against the back wall of his kitchen and went to answer the door. His mail was still being delivered to Esme's, but it could be one of his neighbors or an errant package.

"What the hell have you done?" his father asked by way of a greeting when Ryder opened the door.

"Hey, Dad." Ryder ran a hand through his unwashed hair and wished he'd changed into something besides the T-shirt and athletic shorts he'd slept in. "This is a surprise."

Chandler wore a bright white oxford and tan wool pants instead of his usual dark-colored slacks, a nod to casual Fridays at the office. "I'm sure it's not as big of a surprise as I had. I stopped by Esme Fortune's house this morning."

"Why were you at Esme's? I thought you were in Dallas and Phoenix until the beginning of next week."

The company had recently purchased a property in Arizona nestled in the foothills of the Sedona mountains. Although his father hadn't been scheduled to oversee the transition to a new management team, he'd decided to parlay an overnight trip to Dallas into a week in Arizona.

Ryder had assumed the trip was partially prompted by Chandler's avoidance of Esme and Chase. He didn't know why his dad was so reluctant to meet his second grandson and Esme, but the subtle rejection stung, so he'd stopped issuing invitations.

Didn't it figure that his dad chose the week that Ryder's life imploded to show back up like he'd been ready to take an active interest all along?

"Your timing is absolutely perfect, given how my life is going right now."

Chandler raised a heavy brow. "Are you going to

invite me in, or am I interrupting you watching the morning talk shows?"

Ryder laughed despite the joke falling flat. "As a matter of fact, I just got off the phone with one of the vendors negotiating a new contract. No need to paint me as an underachiever, Dad. I might not have Brandon's slick manner, but the label doesn't fit."

Esme had taught Ryder that he shouldn't have to change who he was to win his father's approval, and he'd be forever grateful for her faith in him.

His dad walked into the apartment and glanced around. "Her house is a hell of a lot homier."

"Agreed. I've got coffee and some stale muffins from the grocery if you want breakfast."

Chandler patted his trim stomach. "Esme made me an omelet while I visited with my grandsons. It was delicious."

"Of course she did," Ryder muttered. Omelets were her specialty. Their routine had been to take turns cooking breakfast on weekend mornings. Omelets on her day and pancakes or waffles when he was in charge of the meal.

"Chase looks like you," Chandler observed as he sat on one of the leather stools in front of the small island.

"You knew that. I texted plenty of pictures, even if you weren't interested in meeting him."

His father's shoulders stiffened. "I'm not sure if you've noticed," he said slowly, "but I haven't had the easiest time accepting that I'm getting on in years.

Being old enough to be a grandfather doesn't exactly impress the ladies."

Ryder wasn't sure if his dad expected him to sympathize, but it had been a crappy week, and he wasn't in the mood to be placating.

"Perhaps it wouldn't be such an issue if you dated women anywhere close to your own age."

His dad laughed and nodded. "You have a valid point, son. Speaking of that, I met someone in Florida a couple of weeks ago. She's a year older than me and out of my league in every way."

"Sounds promising."

Chandler flashed a goofy grin that looked out of place on his serious face. "She is interested in your situation and impressed that I raised a son willing to step up for two children."

A new girlfriend might explain his father's interest in finally meeting Chase and Esme—if the two of them could help him make a good impression on a woman.

"I can see by your face that you don't trust my intentions, and that's also well deserved. But I think it could get serious with Lynda. I convinced her to meet me in Arizona, and I'm hoping she'll come to Texas for bluebonnet season."

"I guess we'll see what happens," Ryder conceded, unsure how to behave with this kinder, gentler version of his father.

"We sure will. In the meantime, the way Lynda talks about the joy her grandchildren bring to her life made me rethink my feelings about being involved in both my grandsons' lives."

Despite the ongoing struggles with his father, Ryder couldn't deny that he wanted Chandler to get to know Chase and Noah.

"I appreciate you making an effort to meet them, Dad…and I don't know how much Esme told you. But things are strained between us at the moment." He blew out a breath. "The fact is, I'm going to need your support. Now more than ever."

"If that's the case, why did I have to hear about the change in your living status from her? Does your brother know? I haven't talked to Brandon since I've been back."

"I haven't told anyone. It's humiliating."

"Hayes men don't deal well with humiliation."

"I suppose." Ryder grabbed his empty coffee mug from the desk and then went to the counter to refill it. "I make terrible coffee compared to Esme. Can I offer you a cup?"

His father nodded. "I'd love some awful coffee. Esme wasn't exactly forthcoming with details. She simply told me the two of you have decided it would be best to live separately until you find a place that gives each of you more privacy. There's nothing humiliating about making an arrangement you didn't ask for work. However you can."

Ryder poured the coffee, then took the carton of half-and-half out of the refrigerator. He poured a generous dollop into his cup. Chandler took his coffee black—like his soul, Ryder used to think when he watched his father gulp down pots of the bitter brew as a child. Now he could see his dad as human, flaws and all, but not the villain Ryder had made him out to be.

"I asked her to marry me," he said after a long sip. "She said no, just like Steph did, so that's the second time I've proposed marriage and been rejected."

"Third time's a charm?" his father suggested with a wry smile.

"Oh, no. There won't be another time. I've learned my lesson. You always told me the Hayes men weren't meant for love, and I think I've proved it more than once."

"Do you love Esme Fortune?"

Had he inadvertently mentioned love? Ryder's heart pounded in his chest. He hadn't meant to say the *L* word. "I should have said the Hayes men are terrible at relationships."

Chandler lifted the cup to his lips, grimacing after taking a drink. "You weren't kidding about brewing horrible coffee. It reminds me of the kind I make. But this business with Esme is different than the mistakes I made with women. Your mom, in particular. Things got tangled up with her, and I couldn't right them."

"Did you ever try?"

"At first," his father asserted. "You were too young to remember, I suppose. But not as much as I could have or should have. Your mother and I married young. She got pregnant immediately, and your brother came a year later. My business was starting to take off, and to be honest, I wasn't ready to settle down."

Chandler put his cup on the counter and shrugged. "So I didn't. It wasn't right, but I can't change the past. You're not like me, Ryder. Me or your brother. You're built like your mother. You were made for commitment. You're steady and sure."

Heat clawed its way up Ryder's neck. He wasn't confident he deserved his father's praise and wasn't used to receiving it.

"You might think I'm built for a serious relationship, but I can't find anyone willing to commit. I should have learned my lesson when Steph crushed my heart."

"Did she truly crush it all that badly? From the bit I saw, the two of you had been tumultuous from the start, and weren't you on a break when she found out she was pregnant?"

Ryder inclined his head. "Yes, but everything changed when she got pregnant. No offense, Dad, but I saw what a loveless marriage looks like for too many years. I decided I was going to love her, and I did. It wasn't enough."

"Son, I've made more than my fair share of mistakes with women over the years, but even I know you can't make yourself love somebody if the feelings aren't there."

Ryder started to bite off a peevish retort, then stopped and thought about his father's words. Had he been in love with Stephanie, or had he been in love with the idea of having a family of his own, one that he could show the care and feeling that his parents had never given to their marriage? He'd been absolutely gutted when she died in the accident, but most of that sadness came from her life being cut short and for his son, who would never know his mother.

"Besides, if you are so dead-set against a love-less marriage," his father continued, "then explain to me again why you proposed to Esme. It seemed like the two of you were rubbing along fine with-out the shackles of a wedding ceremony." Chandler gave a mock shudder. "I don't think you could pay me enough to walk down the aisle again, not that anyone would have me. Anyone worth marrying."

"I didn't want to lose her," Ryder admitted. "Some-thing about walking away from her and Chase when only one parent was allowed to stay overnight at the hospital got to me. I had an overwhelming desire to bind myself to her."

He paused, then added, "But it wasn't done out of love. After Stephanie, I vowed not to let myself love again. I proposed to Esme because I want to build a life together."

"I think you love her," his father said. "And it scares the hell out of you. Which is a trait, unfortu-nately, that you inherited from me."

"You know, she said something similar. Not about me being afraid but the fact that she thinks I love her and won't admit it. It's ridiculous, and too bad she wouldn't talk about it with you. The two of you could have had quite a laugh at my expense. You tell me I don't love the woman I thought I loved, but I do love the woman I can't allow myself to love."

His father looked pained. "I wouldn't laugh at this

situation. I hate that you're hurting and confused. I'm not used to it, Ryder. You always know exactly what to say and do. You're the man with the plan, and we've come to rely on you for that."

"It would appear that either Esme didn't get the memo or that she's unimpressed by my plan."

He lifted the mug to his mouth again, then turned and dumped the coffee into the sink. More caffeine was the last thing he needed. He was already too wired. "It'll work out, Dad. Don't worry about me. I've got my priorities straight."

"I know you do." His father drew one finger along the edge of the counter as if contemplating something serious. "Speaking of priorities, the situation with Esme is not the only reason I'm here."

This was the moment Ryder had been both waiting for and dreading. Chandler had promised to announce his successor at Hayes Enterprises by the end of the month. Despite the weeks Ryder had taken off recently and the fact that he couldn't put in the hours his brother did because being a father came first, he knew he contributed to the company. But he wasn't confident that would be enough to win the CEO position.

"You've made your decision," he said.

Chandler nodded with a smile playing around the corners of his mouth that looked almost smug, which felt unnecessary.

"It's fine, Dad." Ryder rubbed a hand along the back of his neck. "Rip the Band-Aid off. My week can't get any worse."

"Interesting attitude." Chandler's smile widened slightly. "Can it get better?"

It felt like time stood still for an instant.

"Definitely," Ryder answered.

"You and your brother bring different qualities to the table. Your leadership and vision can't be denied, and the staff has complete faith in you."

That sounded promising.

"Your brother, on the other hand, is a gifted negotiator and has the magic touch with our investors. He thrives on travel and meeting new people, so he can function at any of our properties like he's been part of a team for years."

Why did Ryder feel like he was on a dating show he hadn't signed up for, waiting with bated breath to see if he'd be given the final rose?

"Who will make a better CEO?" He didn't bother to clarify that his father was simply making this decision based on his own opinion—because his was the only perspective that mattered.

"I'd like to appoint you as co-CEOs." Chandler held his hands like a maestro directing a symphony orchestra.

Ryder blinked. "You want Brandon and me to work *together*?" He cleared his throat. "Doing the same job?"

"That's the idea behind naming both of you to a CEO role."

"What's the catch? Have you made a deal with a reality show to film us trying to take each other down?" Ryder practically shouted the accusation.

He'd just started to repair his relationship with Brandon. He refused to be pitted against his brother once again.

"No." His father shook his head and rose from the chair, pacing to the edge of the kitchen and then back. "Of all the mistakes I made, fostering that inherent competition between you and Brandon is the one I most regret. You remember me telling you that my brother, Tom, died my senior year of college?"

Ryder nodded. "He was killed in the line of duty."

"A true hero," Chandler said with a nod. "He was two years younger than me, and I wanted nothing to do with him. We played different sports, had separate groups of friends and refused to share our toys. It was so stupid, and once he was gone, I realized how much I missed him. I thought we could keep you close by encouraging—and sometimes demanding—that you and Brandon were interested in the same things, even if you were competing."

"It did *not* keep us close." Ryder laughed softly. "You had to see that, Dad."

"I figured the two of you arguing and vying for the same prizes was better than if you ignored each other, but I've never been great with appropriate emotions or ways of demonstrating them."

Ryder searched for the resentment he usually felt toward his dad but couldn't find it, which felt like its own sort of prize, even more than the CEO position. "Me, neither," he admitted. "But I guess we can both learn." He liked the idea of working with Brandon instead of against him.

Chandler moved closer and pulled Ryder in for a hug. "I don't have a lot of room to give advice on women, son, but I have no doubt Esme Fortune is worth whatever it takes. I hope you can work things out with her."

"Thanks, Dad." Ryder smiled, but it felt more like a grimace. He agreed with his father, but that didn't mean he had it in him to be the man she deserved.

Chapter Sixteen

"You do know that searching for your dream house is supposed to be a happy event?" Lily placed a hand on Esme's arm. "You look like you're about to throw up."

Esme tried for a smile, but it didn't quite take. She'd come to GreatStore to meet up with Lily during her friend's lunch break. They sat in the corner of the café with Esme's laptop open, looking at the two properties she and Ryder were scheduled to tour the following day.

The boys were with him this morning because his father had invited them over for Saturday brunch to celebrate his dad's decision to name Ryder and Brandon co-CEOs of Hayes Enterprises.

Ryder promised that the invitation had also been extended to her, but she'd declined, using the excuse of having plans with a friend. And then she'd quickly had to make plans. It was imperative that she spend as little time as possible with Ryder because every minute they were together chipped away at another piece of her heart.

Not only that, but she also liked Brandon, and more surprisingly, their father. Allowing herself to become close to the Hayes men felt like establishing more bonds that could potentially be broken down the road. She'd taken an immediate shine to Chandler Hayes when he'd stopped by her house. From everything Ryder told her, she hadn't expected to find his intimidating father also charming and sweet, but Chandler had been instantly enamored with Chase, who looked more like his daddy with each passing week.

Chandler displayed the same amount of affection for Noah, and the quickest way to win Esme over was kindness toward both her babies. Maybe she should blame them for the fact that she'd fallen in love with Ryder, although the reason why didn't matter at this point. Her current dilemma was figuring out how to make herself fall *out* of love with him.

"Neither of these is my dream house." She blinked rapidly and tried to pretend like she wasn't on the verge of tears. "The good news is either will be great for raising boys." She tapped on the laptop screen. "One of them even has a barn on the property. Asa has already threatened to get Chase and Noah ponies for their first birthday."

Lily laughed. "That sounds like Asa. He sure does

love horses, especially Major. He talks about that animal the way proud parents coming into the baby department talk about their children."

"Yeah," Esme agreed. "Major has been with him a long time. The horse is his best friend and possibly the love of his life."

Lily made a face. "The love of his life, huh? That's interesting, to say the least."

Esme smiled despite her aching heart. "Thank you for spending your lunch hour looking at houses with me. I know I should be grateful that Ryder is such a good father to the boys and willing to go in on a house with me. It will make it easier to share parenting duties."

Lily waved as one of her coworkers walked by. As usual on a weekend, the store was crowded, although Esme was glad the Valentine's Day decorations had been taken down. Every time she thought about the perfect date she'd shared with Ryder at Remi's Reads, it made her wish things had turned out differently.

"I don't think it's necessarily easy to be friends with someone when you secretly want more," Lily said softly, and Esme caught the wistful edge in her friend's voice.

"You're right." Esme kept her gaze on the laptop screen. "But I don't regret telling Ryder how I feel. I heard Wendell say that secrets cause more trouble than they're worth, and I agree."

"But when he didn't know, you weren't hurt," Lily countered.

"I also wasn't happy, not completely anyway.

Falling in love with Ryder was a gift, even though it didn't turn out the way I wanted. I thought that a disastrous marriage had ruined my heart." She rubbed two fingers against her chest, covered by the oversize sweatshirt she wore. "But it was still there, bruised but not broken. That's a powerful thing to know about myself. It will take a while, but I'll heal from this heartbreak, too. I have to for the sake of my boys."

"Do you think you'll be ready to date again soon?"

Esme laughed and vehemently shook her head. "Oh, no. I still believe in love, but there's no point in fooling myself. It's going to take a long time to get over Ryder Hayes, if I *ever* do."

"Maybe there's still a chance for the two of you," Lily suggested. "After all, you'll be with him more than you won't." She hit the arrow key to move through the interior photos of one of the potential houses. "Even if you're sleeping on opposite ends of a house. I just wish you could find your dream home. Loving where you live feels important somehow."

Esme drew in a deep breath. "Funny you mention that." She moved the computer's cursor to the browser icon and scrolled to one of her previous searches. "It's not the right house for Ryder and me to share given our current circumstances, but..."

She shifted closer to her friend. "Take a look at this house. It popped up as a new listing yesterday. I'm not sure why it showed up in my search."

Her stomach felt tied in knots as she read the property's description out loud to Lily. Esme had looked at it so many times since the house came on the market the previous day, she practically knew it by heart. "'Turn of the century charm meets modern luxury. This four bedroom, five bath, old homestead ranch stunner has a gourmet kitchen that will welcome family and friends alike. The main-floor primary bedroom has his and her walk-in closets with an en suite bathroom that boasts a steam shower and double vanity. Each of the second-floor bedrooms includes connected bathrooms, high ceilings and window seats perfect for enjoying the view of the open plains.'"

"Is that a library?" Lily asked, grinning at Esme as she pointed at the screen. "It would be perfect for you."

"Can you believe it? If someone had built the house I dreamed of when I was a girl, this would be it. Only I'm not a little girl anymore." She swiped at her cheeks when a few errant tears spilled over. "I know I shouldn't want the fantasy. My heart was frozen after my marriage ended, but it melted for Ryder. I'm not going to close it off again, even if love isn't in the cards for me right now."

"I wish it were," Lily told her with a sympathetic smile.

"It's okay. I should be grateful for the happiness I do have. Chase's health scare showed me that I can't take the good things in my life for granted."

"Of course not," Lily agreed. "You would never do that, but it's also okay to want some things for yourself."

"I wanted Ryder, and that blew up in my face."

"Ryder is an idiot," Lily said simply, and Esme threw an arm around her friend's shoulder.

"That's just what I needed to hear. But I'm in charge of my own happiness and always have been. I've always managed to find a way to be happy." She released a wistful sigh. "And so what if my dream house is for sale in the town that feels like home to me. I'll just use a spare bedroom in whatever house we buy to create my own library."

"That's right. You *are* in charge of your destiny, Esme Fortune."

"What's all this talk about destiny?"

Lily jumped about three feet in the air, and Esme snapped shut the laptop as Asa took a seat across from the two of them.

"What are you lovely ladies doing today?" Asa tapped a finger on the laptop case. "You closed that pretty quickly, little sis. Don't tell me you're setting up your online dating profile already. No, wait. Do tell me because it would serve Ryder Hayes right to have to watch you go out with another man so soon after he mucked up his chance with you."

"Asa, I'm not—"

"I can help weed out the weirdos if you want. Here's a hint, if a guy poses with his guinea pig, both of them dressed in leather chaps, he's probably not the man for you."

Esme and Lily laughed at Asa's silly joke.

"I'm not planning to date anytime soon," she assured her brother. She couldn't imagine any man filling the Ryder-size hole in her heart. But as she'd told Lily, Esme was grateful that these past few weeks had shown her she could love again. She hadn't been sure that was possible but now hoped her heart would eventually mend again.

"Besides, I don't think you have any room to talk. Right, Lily? Asa would probably make his profile picture a selfie of him and Major."

Lily, who normally had no problem joking with Esme, seemed a bit tongue-tied at the moment.

"Major is a fine horse," she said softly.

Esme groaned while her brother reached across the table to high-five her friend.

"He's the best," Asa agreed. "I'm not joining any matchmaking sites. I don't exactly have trouble finding my own dates, if you know what I mean."

"Just trouble keeping them around," Esme teased, then lightly kicked his shin under the table. "*Love 'em and leave 'em cowboy* would be your perfect online username."

"I always leave them happy." Asa wiggled his brows. "Very happy, for the record."

Lily had lifted the cup of coffee she'd ordered to her lips and choked on the sip she'd just taken.

"Stop that," Esme scolded her brother. "You're going to make my friend upchuck, and my corneas are burning at that mental image."

Asa chuckled and handed Lily a napkin. "Sorry about that."

"No problem," she said, her voice strained.

"On the subject of happy…" Asa pumped a fist in

the air. "I think I've finally convinced Val that I'm the ideal buyer for the dude ranch."

Esme felt her eyes widen. "That's great news, but you must be losing your touch if she's not agreed to sell to you already."

"I know, right?" Asa agreed good-naturedly. "But it's going to be worth all the effort I've put in when it's finally mine. The Chatelaine Dude Ranch is special."

"Very special." Lily's smile was tinged with sadness. Esme patted her friend's arm, then shifted her gaze to Asa. "Did you know Lily's family visited the dude ranch when she was a baby?"

Asa frowned like he was trying to place that conversation. "I think you mentioned that," he told Lily.

"I don't have specific memories," she said, holding tight to the coffee cup. "My sisters and I were only ten months old at the time. But I know the dude ranch was a special place even back then. I'm sure once you make it your own, it's going to be really great again."

Esme felt like there was something her friend wasn't sharing about her memories of the dude ranch. Lily's explanation seemed to satisfy Asa, however, who whipped out his phone and began describing the plans he had for the property to the two of them.

Lily nodded and offered words of encouragement, making Esme wonder once again why some great guy hadn't fallen for this sweet woman. Although she had no basis to act as an expert on love at this point, Esme thought any man would be lucky to have Lily love him.

When her lunch break was over, Lily said goodbye before returning to the baby section, and Esme and Asa walked out to the parking lot together. It was a chilly day, although the sun was out. Esme lifted her head to bask in the warmth of it.

"Are you sure you're okay?" Asa asked, gently nudging her. "I know the situation with Ryder has been tough. I'll still kick his butt if you want."

"No need for that," she assured her brother. "I'll be fine. Chatelaine is my home now, and no matter what happens with Ryder and me, that isn't going to change. I'll manage, and I can't wait to see you and Bea achieve your dreams."

"With significant monetary help from Freya Fortune," Asa added wryly.

"I hope as time goes by she starts to feel close to us in more ways than just financially. It was nice of her to help with Noah when Chase was in the hospital, although she seemed freaked out in the Grammy Freya role."

"She'll get there, Es. I'm glad you're doing okay, given everything you've been through." He squeezed her shoulder. "For the record, I highly recommend steering clear of love. It's a lot easier."

She patted his cheek. "One day, Asa, I hope you'll see that even the hard parts are worth it." At least, that was what she was determined to believe.

Ryder sat on one of the leather recliners in his father's giant family room with Noah nestled against his chest. Brandon sat on the matching couch, bouncing Chase on his knee as the baby gurgled happily.

He and his brother made eye contact at the sound of their father laughing from the kitchen, where he'd excused himself to take a call from his new girlfriend, Lynda.

"He sounds giddy," Brandon said, making a face. "It's not right."

Ryder chuckled and stroked a hand over Noah's back. He knew someday his sons would be too big and rambunctious to nap on dear old Dad's lap, so he was going to savor every moment.

"He sounds happy, which is a definite change. I think it's a good one."

Brandon nodded. "Dad's a lot happier than you, given the recent change in your living situation." He lifted Chase to eye level. "Can you explain to me, little one, why your adoring uncle Brandon had to hear from Grandpa about Daddy royally messing up with Mommy?

"Because Daddy is an idiot." Brandon answered his own question in a childlike voice as if it were Chase speaking.

"Very funny," Ryder muttered. "But no son of mine will call me an idiot."

"Both of them will eventually call you worse if you don't patch things up with Esme."

"Not that it's any of your business, *Uncle Brandon*, or that you have any room to talk when it comes to long-term relationships, but there's nothing to patch up. Esme and I are fine."

"Dude, you look miserable, especially given that we are finally getting a chance to make our mark on Hayes Enterprises and doing it together. I know it's not the thought of working with me that has you perpetually scowling."

Ryder rolled his eyes. "Are you sure?"

Brandon flipped him a middle finger accompanied by a wide smile. "You were always too serious, but she lightened you up, Ry. Esme did a whole world of good in your life. And being my co-CEO is probably the best thing that ever happened to you career-wise."

"So modest, but right back at you," Ryder said with an attempt at laughter that sounded more like a grunt. "Besides, Esme is still a part of my life. It's just different. We're going to look at properties tomorrow, so once we close on a new place, we'll move in, and then it will feel normal again."

"Only *different* isn't good in this case," his brother insisted. "You aren't happy, Ryder."

"I'm fine."

Brandon sat up straighter and pulled Chase close to his chest as he stared at Ryder. "I can't decide if you're just lying to me or if you hope to convince yourself to believe the lie as well. Listen to Dad in there. If he can pull it out after all these years, then you've got a great chance of fixing things with Esme."

He shook his head. "How am I supposed to fix things with a woman who doesn't want me? I don't know why everybody thinks this is my fault. She's the one who ended it with me. I wanted to marry her."

"She wanted you to love her."

Nerves skittered through Ryder like centipedes crawling over his skin. Unable to sit still, he rose from the chair and started pacing back and forth. Noah made a sound of protest before settling back against his chest again.

"You know I can't do that. I tried to love Steph, and it made things worse. Why would I risk that with Esme? She's too important. I lo…" He shook his head. "Never mind."

Brandon pointed at Ryder, then touched the tip of his finger to his nose. "That's it exactly. You were going to say you love her."

"Was not," Ryder muttered.

"You *love* her," Brandon repeated, "and you don't even have to try. It just happened. You weren't planning on it, and it scares you. I get that."

"How do you get it?" Ryder demanded. "You ever been in love?"

Brandon shook his head and looked uncharacteristically somber. "No, but I'd like to experience it, especially with somebody as well suited to me as Esme is to you. Don't you see? This is the ultimate prize."

Ryder shot him a glare. "Wait. Are you saying that I've screwed it up, so now you're going to try to make a move on Esme? Because that's a terrible idea, Bran."

"First, I'm offended you would suggest that, although I understand my history with your girlfriends isn't stellar. I wouldn't do something like that now, and even if I did, Esme is head over heels in love with you, buddy. I've seen how she looks at you and how giddy she gets when you smile at her. At least admit to yourself that you love her too because it's pretty dang obvious to the rest of us."

Ryder could hardly breathe around the emotion swelling in his chest. "Of course, I love her," he said quietly. "But what good does it do me other than create the potential for experiencing more pain? This can't just be about the two of us. The boys are involved, so if I mess it up, there's way more at stake than my heart. The last thing I want is to hurt her or our sons."

"I hate to be the one to break it to you, bro. But that train has left the station. You did hurt her, but she's willing to put aside her feelings for the sake of Chase and Noah. Imagine what could happen if you took the risk. It's not going to get worse, but it sure could get a hell of a lot better if you tell her how you feel and stop letting fear run the show."

Ryder closed his eyes and let the fear wash over him. His fear of being hurt and being rejected—of being alone. But the biggest fear of all was losing Esme.

What if she met somebody else? What if he had to watch her with another guy?

Noah wriggled in his arms, and he wondered if the baby could feel Ryder's heart thundering in his chest. "Am I the biggest idiot on the planet?" Ryder asked the baby.

"Quite possibly," Brandon answered in his pretend child's voice.

"Rhetorical question," he muttered.

"The better question is, what are you going to do about it?"

Chandler walked into the room at that moment. "What did I miss?" he demanded as his gaze moved between his sons.

"I love Esme," Ryder said quietly.

"Yes, I know, son." His father nodded. "It's about time you figured it out."

And now that he had, Ryder needed to find a way to convince her to give him another chance.

Chapter Seventeen

When the doorbell rang an hour later, Esme assumed it was Ryder home with the boys. He'd insisted on returning her house key to her, even though she'd told him to keep it.

"Hi, Esme," Ruby Ashwood said as she held up a hand in a nervous wave. "Is this a bad time? I was hoping to talk to you for a minute."

"This is a fine time," Esme said. She wasn't certain why the hairs on her arm stood on end and a slight shiver passed through her. She took a step back to let Ruby enter. "Ryder took Chase and Noah to visit their grandpa. They should be back soon."

Ruby blew out a breath. "I'm relieved to get the chance to talk to you one-on-one. Ryder is super handsome, but he's kind of intense. The guy doesn't smile much, does he?"

To Esme, it felt like he smiled all the time. Maybe she projected that on him, or perhaps he saved his smiles for her. "He laughs at the boys often enough." She supposed she had no reason to be loyal to him anymore, but it was her nature when she loved someone. That was how she knew her heartache over her late husband had been more about his betrayal than the loss of him.

"Would you like a glass of water? Or I made lemon poppyseed muffins yesterday."

"Water would be great, but I can't eat anything right now." Ruby wrapped her arms around her waist. "My stomach is tied up in too many knots."

"Is everything okay? How's your grandma?"

Esme walked into the kitchen with the young woman following her.

"She's the one who told me I should come and talk to you."

"Have a seat at the table." Esme took two glasses from the cabinet, filled them with ice and then turned on the tap. "If you're here to apologize, you don't owe me anything, Ruby. We're good."

A horrifying thought streaked a trail across her mind like a firework in the sky, bright and terrible with its whistle reverberating through her chest. "If Ryder reached out to you…"

"Nothing like that. I haven't talked to him since that day when he interviewed my grandma and me. It's probably a blessing that he never called. Honestly, he was a safe guy to flirt with and give my number to. It was clear he only had eyes for you."

"We're not together like that." Esme set the two glasses of water on the table. "Not anymore."

Ruby gripped the glass but didn't take a drink. "Really? I thought the two of you were the real deal. It was cute how you guys kept looking at each other like you were truly together."

"We're partners in co-parenting. There's just—"

"I think I was the one who messed up the ID bracelets," Ruby blurted.

Esme blinked. The young nursing assistant could have knocked her over with a feather.

"I don't understand. You seemed certain it wasn't you when we talked to you and your grandma."

"A lot was going on that night, you know?"

Esme definitely knew.

"I mean, there was the storm, and then the regular L-and-D floor flooded, and we had to move you all down. It was my first week, and moms were screaming, and babies were crying. There was one mom in particular who was so loud. Nana said it was your other baby's mom. I was new, and at first, one of the other nurses was putting the ID bracelets on the ankles. Then she got called out for an emergency."

Ruby took a drink, her fingers shaking. "The thing that jogged my memory is that you and Ryder kept asking about the other volunteer. Not my grandma, but the woman who never came back after that night. I didn't remember her at first, but after talking to you two, it started coming back to me." She released a breath and gave Esme a pained look. "Honestly, after I got off that shift, I went over to

The Corral and drank way too much. I didn't remember much of anything the next day, and frankly, I didn't want to. But I can picture that woman's eyes. They were so blue, like the color of bluebonnets. I'd never seen anyone with eyes like that, and she was there."

Esme felt her chest pinch. She placed her hands on the table as if the wood might ground her.

"She wasn't doing the same job as me," Ruby explained. "But I remember her standing in the doorway to the room we were using to do the footprints, bracelets and such. It was more like an oversize storage closet. She was staring like she knew something about me. I got pretty flustered and...well... I'm here to admit my mistake."

After all the worry, Esme had almost no physical or emotional reaction to solving the mystery of who had switched the ID bracelets. It made sense, and Ruby seemed to be telling the truth as she remembered it.

Had the mystery volunteer, whoever she was, seen the mistake and not said anything? Esme couldn't imagine it, but maybe that volunteer had been as shaken by that night as Ruby seemed to be.

"Say something, Esme," Ruby pleaded. "I'm so sorry. If you and Ryder want to sue me or something, I understand. I don't have much, but—"

"No. We wanted to know what happened the night Chase and Noah were born. Now we do."

"I'm so sorry," Ruby repeated. "I wish y'all could find the old woman. Maybe she'd remember something more. She had a cane and didn't walk well, so she could have had bad eyesight. Likely she didn't even realize what I was doing."

"I appreciate you coming here to tell me. Ryder will, too."

"He's gonna be so mad," Ruby said with a frown. "I hate people being mad at me, but I guess I deserve it."

"He'll be glad we don't have to keep searching for an answer," Esme assured the younger woman.

"Just so you know, I quit my job at the hospital. My grandma was right—I got my CNA license because of a crush on a doctor. I thought if I worked in the hospital, he would see me as a viable love interest. He started dating one of the scrub techs over at County—one of the male scrub techs, so I never had a shot."

"That's a tough break," Esme said, still processing Ruby's revelation as the woman continued to speak.

"My grandma also wanted me to do something meaningful with my life, but after this, she said she just wants me to be happy. So I'm going to nail school."

She held out her hands to display her nails, painted a milky pink. "I'm going to specialize in gel manicures. They're really popular. I like a natural look, but I can do whatever. If you ever want a manicure, I'll gladly give you one for free. In fact, you can have free manicures for the rest of your life because there's nothing I can do to make up for what happened with your babies."

"I swear it's okay, Ruby." Esme realized she truly meant the words. "Maybe the switch was destined to happen because I was meant to be a mother to both of my boys."

Ruby's frown quickly transformed into a smile. "That's a nice way of looking at it. Those two babies are lucky to have you. Ryder Hayes, too. I hope y'all work things out."

Esme had given up on hope, at least for herself.

"Good luck with nail school, Ruby. I know it's not the same as nursing, but you're going to make women feel pretty and pampered. There's not enough of that in the world these days."

The young woman got up and came around the table to hug Esme. "Thank you for being so nice and for saying that."

Esme said goodbye to Ruby, closed the door and then stood in the center of her family room. Her future was the result of an innocent mistake by a frazzled hospital employee. Now she knew the truth, but what did it change?

Not her love for either of her babies or, as she'd told Ruby, the fact that she loved being a mother to both of them. Esme was grateful for her sons and the unconventional family she and Ryder shared.

The front door opened, and she must have had quite the look on her face because Ryder immediately stopped.

"I'm sorry. Do you want me to knock? I know this is all new."

She shook her head and ran a hand over her cheek,

surprised to find her body still solid when it felt like she was one million particles floating through the air.

Ryder picked up Noah's infant seat, which he'd set on the porch while he opened the door and stepped inside. "Did I see that nursing assistant we talked to driving away?"

"Yes." Esme stepped forward and closed the door behind him. "Sit down, Ryder. There's something I need to tell you..."

Ryder's emotions had run the gamut in the past twelve hours, from panic at Esme's wide eyes and serious tone when she'd told him she had something to share, to relief that the mystery of Chase and Noah's switch finally had a resolution.

A thin trickle of hope had followed like a mountain stream in the spring, flowing as the ice and snow above it melted. That was one of the many gifts Esme had given him—melting his heart and allowing him to believe in love again.

Or maybe it was for the first time. He'd wanted things to work with Steph for the sake of their son, but he could see now that trying to convince himself that a sense of duty could transform into love had been naive. Falling for Esme had been easy— they were like two pieces of a puzzle that fit together perfectly.

But he'd hurt her, and any plan he'd had to beg her to try again felt weak and insignificant after she'd explained what Ruby had shared. Although she'd seemed pleased to know the truth, her eyes had remained guarded, her manner distant, like she'd resigned herself to the idea of nothing more between them.

So he'd locked down the declaration he wanted to make, telling himself he needed to give her time.

But another sleepless night convinced him that there was no way he could hold off any longer. He didn't want to wait, even though he had no way of knowing how she'd respond.

Esme had taken a risk in sharing her heart, and he owed her that same courage but had no clue how to prove his devotion until he'd stopped by Great-Store on the way to her house to pick up a few things for the boys.

He'd seen Lily Perry working in the baby department. Whether from lack of sleep, desperation or a combination of the two, Ryder had asked Esme's friend for advice. The request had seemed to shock them both, but one thing Esme had taught Ryder was that he didn't have to handle everything on his own and pretend he had it all together when he was a jumbled mess on the inside.

Lily had fired off a barrage of questions about Ryder's intentions, clearly protective of her friend, just like Esme's sister had been weeks earlier. It made him feel equally grateful and embarrassed. He should be the one to be protecting Esme, and he would for the rest of his life if she'd give him another shot.

His answers must have satisfied Lily because, after a few moments, she'd pulled out her phone and pulled up the site for the realty company he and Esme were working with, assuring him that his best chance of achieving a future with Esme would be to make her secret wish come true.

If Freya Fortune could be a wish maker, Ryder would take a page from the older woman's playbook and do the same. He only hoped it would be enough.

"I think you missed the turn," Esme said with a frown as she pointed to the street they'd just passed.

"There's something I need to pick up at my dad's," Ryder answered. "It will be a quick stop at the gated community."

"Oh." She glanced at her watch. "I don't want to be late for our appointment. The Realtor said there's another family interested in the property."

"We'll be right on time," he assured her, then cleared his throat after his voice cracked on the last word like he was a gangly teenager. He certainly felt as nervous as one, and the fact that Esme had indirectly referred to them as a family made emotion blossom in his chest in the best way possible.

He waved to the man at the guard stand, who recognized Ryder's car and buzzed them in. As he drove through the quiet streets, it felt like ribbons of hope fluttered across his heart.

She watched out the passenger window after turning to check on the boys, each of whom was happily playing with the toys hanging from the handle of their respective car seats.

"I thought your dad lived on the other side of the neighborhood," she said as Ryder turned onto a cul-de-sac with about a half dozen houses. A perfect street for a family.

He heard Esme's breath catch as he pulled into the driveway of the house at the end, a white-washed brick structure with shutters painted black and a wraparound front porch with a view of the lake across the street.

She gazed at the house briefly before turning to face him. "Ryder, where are we?"

He flashed a smile and reached for her hand. "I hope we're home."

Esme climbed out of the car, unable to take her gaze off the house she found perfect in every way, and placed two fingers to her heart. If she pressed hard enough, maybe she could force her emotions back into the place where she'd tried to stuff them after that conversation where Ryder offered her the future she wished for as his wife, but in a way that made it impossible to accept.

It felt like an eerily similar situation with the house. She didn't understand how he'd known to take her here, but her dream was in front of her yet still out of reach because there was no way she could make a home there and keep her heart from breaking all over again every single day.

He came to stand beside her, and she could feel him studying her expression. "What's wrong? Is this not the right one? Lily showed me the listing and told me this was the house you loved, so I called the Realtor. If there's a different one—"

"Why are we here?" Esme asked, barely recognizing her own hollow voice. She turned to him, not bothering to hide the tears she felt filling her eyes. His eyes were the color of grass after a spring rain— so full of life and promise that it almost hurt her to look at him.

"I can't live here with you," she whispered, willing him to understand without the humiliation of having to explain it outright.

"I'm sorry," he said automatically.

She turned toward the car, placing one hand on the door handle. "It's okay. Let's get out of here before the Realtor arrives. You can text her and—"

"I'm sorry for being such a fool," Ryder clarified. "I've said it before, Esme. You're better than me in every way, so when you told me you love me, I was terrified."

She turned slowly. "The thought of me loving you is terrifying?"

He nodded, then quickly shook his head. "Yes, but not in the way you think. I know I don't deserve you. I spent my whole life striving to make people happy and earn love. First, with my parents, particularly my father. And then Steph. Nothing I did was good enough. Nothing worked. Then you came along and loved me with no strings, like your heart was mine for the taking."

"It was," she confirmed. "Only you didn't want it. Just like my parents, who were too wrapped up in themselves to care about being loved by their children, and like Seth, who didn't value what I had to offer him. I can't do it anymore, Ryder. I can't keep giving my heart to people who won't take care of it."

"But I will, Esme. I can't promise I won't be scared, but if you give me another chance, I will hold and cherish your heart. I love you, Esme. I will love you forever."

"You love me," she murmured. The words turned over in her mind—wildflower seeds floating on the breeze until they landed in her heart like they'd found a home. She would nurture his love the way he promised to take care of her heart.

"I do," he said. "Do you think you could love me again?"

She laughed softly. "I never stopped, Ryder, and despite what I told myself, I don't think I ever could. I dreamed of a happily-ever-after but didn't understand the effort it would take. Now I do, and there's no one I'd rather spend my life partnering with than you. I love who you are as a man and a father. I'll give you *all* the chances."

He leaned in and kissed her passionately, sealing their promise to each other. But before she could say anything more, he took a velvet box from his pocket and dropped to one knee in front of her.

"I don't want to hurry you," he said with a hopeful smile. "But I also don't want to wait. Will you marry me, Esme Fortune? You are my life and my love. You and the boys are already my family. My heart. Would you do me the honor of making it official?"

Joy bloomed inside her, bright and fizzy like champagne bubbles. "Yes," she told him as he slipped a brilliant yellow-hued diamond ring on her left hand. "Yes, I'll marry you, Ryder."

He stood to wrap his arms around her. "I never realized I could be this happy."

"Especially not as a result of a mistake like the one that brought us together," she said before he kissed her again.

"Not a mistake." He pulled back and opened the car's back door to reveal Noah and Chase sleeping soundly in their infant seats. "A miracle. Our two miracles."

"Our two miracles," she agreed, knowing whatever adventures life brought their way, she and Ryder would handle them together. Always.

* * * * *

Don't miss Asa Fortune's story,
Fortune in Name Only
Available February 2024 from Harlequin!

When Asa Fortune is told he needs a wife to buy his dream ranch, he never expected his best friend, Lily Perry, to agree to a six-month marriage! But as the pair makes the ranch a true home, can they admit that they've found their oasis...in one another?

#3035 THE COWBOY'S ROAD TRIP
Men of the West • by Stella Bagwell

When introverted rancher Kipp Starr agrees to join Beatrice Hollister on a road trip, he doesn't plan on being snowbound and stranded with his sister's outgoing sister-in-law. Or falling in love with her.

#3036 THE PILOT'S SECRET
Cape Cardinale • by Allison Leigh

Former aviator Meyer Cartell just inherited a decrepit beach house—and his nearest neighbor is thorny nurse Sophie Lane. Everywhere he turns, the young—and impossibly attractive—Sophie is there...holding firm to her old grudge against him. Until his passionate kisses convince her otherwise.

#3037 FLIRTING WITH DISASTER
Hatchet Lake • by Elizabeth Hrib

When Sarah Schaffer packs up her life and her two-year-old son following the completion of her travel-nursing contract, she's not prepared for former army medic turned contractor Desmond Torres to catch her eye. Or for their partnership in rebuilding a storm-damaged town to heal her guarded heart.

#3038 TWENTY-EIGHT DATES
Seven Brides for Seven Brothers • by Michelle Lindo-Rice

Courtney Meadows needs a hero—and Officer Brigg Harrington is happy to oblige. He gives the very pregnant widow a safe haven during a hurricane. But between Brigg's protective demeanor and heated glances, Courtney's whirlwind emotions are her biggest challenge yet.